SIW Goes

PLATINUM

**Other Titles by
The Southern Indiana Writers' Group**

The Indian Creek Anthology Series:

Indian Creek Anthology
Ghost Writers
Christmas Bizarre
Dragon: Our Tales
Grounds for Suspicion
2000 Tales
Way Out West
Unbridled Lust
There's Something Under the Bedtime Stories
Novel Ingredients
Write of Passage
Off the Rack
Beastly Tales
It's Always Something
Most Wanted
Future Perfect: Tense in Space
Holiday Bizarre
Pair of Normal What?
The Worst Book in the Universe

Also by SIW:

Ghosts: On the Square . . . And Elsewhere. . . .

Visit The authors at:
southernindianawriters.com

SIW Goes

PLATINUM

Southern Indiana Writers' Group

Per Bastet

XX SIW Goes Platinum
Volume 20 of the Indian Creek Anthology Series

Published by Per Bastet LLC, P.O. Box 3023 Corydon, IN 47112

Cover art by T. Lee Harris

ISBN 978-1-942166-18-4

SIW Goes

PLATINUM

Contents

Foreword

And they said it wouldn't last.

The Southern Indiana Writers Group has been together for more than two decades. This volume marks our twentieth themed anthology. As always, our "theme" has been pretty broadly interpreted by our eclectic band: Twenty, platinum, X, XX, cross, double-cross. . . . This group tends to push the envelope until the glue melts and the flaps come off. The group, itself, nevertheless, and to the astonishment of all, holds together.

Marian Allen
Sept. 21, 2016

X marks the Spot
Brenda Drexler

X marks the spot.
What spot?
That spot.
How do you know it's that spot?
Because that's the spot.
THE spot?
Yes, THE spot.
Hmm. What if there are two spots? Would you need two x's?
I don't know, maybe, I guess.
Then it couldn't be THE spot, because then there would be two spots.
Not true.
There can only be one THE of anything, therefore, only one THE spot.
I agree wholeheartedly.
Hmm. Then how do you know if it is THE spot and not just any spot?
Because it has an X on it. Like I said, X marks THE spot.
Who marks THE spot?
Anybody, I guess.
How does anybody actually know it's THE spot?

They just do. They recognize it as THE spot and mark it with an X.

What makes one spot THE spot as opposed to just any old spot?

There is something special about that spot so they mark it with an X so everyone will know it's THE spot.

Hmm, everyone? Doesn't seem it would be so special if everyone knows it.

Well, everyone doesn't usually recognize it for THE Spot. They have to find a spot with an X on it, then they know.

Then what?

What do you mean, 'then what'?

What do we do if we find THAT Spot?

It's THE Spot.

You are playing with technicalities, now, trying to confuse the truth.

The truth? You can't handle the truth.

I think the truth is that you don't know what you're talking about.

Truth is relative, my friend. You can have yours and I can have mine.

So I can have my spot and you can have yours?

Of course. That is reasonable.

Then you can have an X to mark your spot and I can have my X.

Of course.

Aha! That's my point. THE X for THE SPOT. There is only one THE anything.

I will gladly discuss this until you understand, poor fellow.

Who are you, anyway?

Aristotle.

THE Aristotle?

What do you think?

I think you're a mad man.

Au contraire, compere. Why can I not be THE Aristotle? Am I not standing on THE Spot?

I can't see the spot.

That's because I am standing on it. Wouldn't that be reasonable?

I don't know.

Ah, I know.

An Evening With Coatlicue

T. Lee Harris

From Josh Katzen's perspective in the taxi, it looked like half the participants of the Conference on Central and South American Archaeology were staying at the same hotel he was. No surprise, really. It was one of the closest to the actual convention center and one of the best in that part of downtown Mexico City. His problem was that it also looked like the archaeologists were having a pre-conference meet-and-greet between him and the the lobby entrance and, at the moment, he was heartily sick of archaeologists. Well, one archaeologist in particular, but it was gratifying to swing the wide brush.

He'd get over it, but he was fresh from the convention center's lecture hall where he'd spent the last two hours with Dr. Avi Rosenberg tweaking a slide show about the latest finds at the Piedras Rojas dig in Peru. He considered it a lost hour — maybe hour and a half. The presentation was working fine, but Rosenberg was stressing out over this one. Why? Who knew. You'd think after being an instructor for a dog's age, having presented papers to other international conferences and even being on TV, the man wouldn't think twice about doing a lecture. Nope. Not this time.

Katzen exited the taxi and shouldered his way through the kibitzing throng toward an inviting open space just in front of the hotel's bank of etched glass doors. Hand on the fancy bronze door pull, he sneaked a peek at his watch before entering. Was there enough time to hit one of the museums? There were several good ones close by and he'd hate to come to Mexico City only to waste the whole first day futzing around, waiting for an experienced lecturer to get over a case of butterflies. Truth to tell, the butterflies might well be on their way to eviction, anyway. When he'd left Avi at the convention center, he'd been deep in an animated discussion with several colleagues on the pros and cons of digital recording versus old-school hand-drawing. Rosenberg favored a mixture of both.

There was a touch on his arm and someone behind him said, "Durand. . . ?"

Surprised at hearing the name, he turned to see a tall man of medium build with short, dark hair giving way to gray. The man's face registered amazed recognition.

There was a moment of recognition on Katzen's part, too. A niggling recollection from another time, another life. Another recollection in the back of his head didn't niggle. It screamed, "CIA".

Not noticing the hesitation, the man continued, "It *is* you. The Cat. Damn. Rumor has it that you were killed." Abruptly, the man's narrow face spasmed. He staggered forward, falling heavily against Katzen, bearing them both to the ground behind one of the massive stone-clad columns of the hotel facade.

For a few beats, they lay face-to-face in a ghastly parody of a romantic embrace until the dark-haired man rolled over into a sitting position, back against the pillar. He croaked something close to a laugh, his lips moister and redder than before. "Looks like the rumor mill has the wrong one of us killed, Major."

Katzen was still playing mental catch-up as the CIA agent groaned and shoved a small, brown paper-wrapped bundle into his hands. "Good thing I ran into you, Cat. Hand-off here is screwed. Take this. Get to Aureole by twenty hundred hours. Lobby. Red shirt. Times." He convulsed, then went still.

The crowd had been slow to notice what happened, but they were starting to react now. Katzen heard a flurry of gasped "Oh my god"s and murmured "What's going on"s. Two uniformed security guards pushed their way through. One stood slightly behind him while the other requested an ambulance via his shoulder comm.

The guard looked from the body to Katzen. "What has happened, señor?"

"I don't know," Katzen said, even though he had a nasty feeling he did. Gingerly lifting the fallen man's jacket aside he found verification in the form of a dark puddle oozing into the back of the garment.

The guard saw it, too, and his hand flew to his comm. "Dispatch! We have a man shot at the North—" He broke off, staring in confusion at the red stain spreading across his uniform front. A second later, he crumpled to the pavement.

This time the crowd noticed. Someone shouted, "GUN!" just as something zipped through Katzen's hair. Stone dust sprayed from the polished granite beside him and he blinked reflexively as blown-back shards stung his face. He wasted a nano-second before diving for the lobby doors. His fingertips had barely brushed the bronze pulls when the elegant plate glass shivered and exploded.

Shit. They're shooting at ME!

The crowd became a mob. People screamed. They

prayed and sobbed and ran in every conceivable direction. The remaining security guard plastered himself behind a column, shouting into his comm, side arm out.

Katzen plunged through the gaping hole left by the shattered door and rolled to the side, putting the solid stone wall between himself and the sniper as another bullet skipped and sparked off the marble flooring of the grand entry, barely missing the panicked people inside. Coming to his feet, he crouch-ran for the hallway that led deeper into the hotel complex. It was tough going until he ducked into a stairwell and closed the door against the chaos outside.

Sirens rose above the screams as he reached his floor. Bolting into his room, he pulled the drapes then backed several yards away from the windows and stood, taking slow, deep breaths. It took longer than he liked to overcome the adrenaline rush.

Okay. Okay. It was a sniper. That much was clear. The interval between the first and second shots must have been the shooter changing position after he and the CIA agent fell behind the cover of the pillar. The second shot took out the security guard who was standing right behind him. The man must have been in the way. A deadly case of wrong place, wrong time. After that, the shots seemed to be aimed strictly at *him*. Why? Did the shooter see the agent transfer the — *package*. He'd almost forgotten about the package even though he'd been clenching it in his fist the whole time. Maybe whatever was in there would explain what just happened.

Taking the bundle to the desk, he carefully removed the brown paper, revealing a small jade figurine of Coatlicue, the Aztec earth goddess. It was small. Between three and four inches — it fitted well across the palm of his hand. The goddess' skull-like face, with its circles of turquoise inset into the cheekbones beneath hollow eye sockets, was uplifted. Claw-like hands were raised shoulder high, palms outward. Flaccid breasts drooped to meet the belt of her signature knee-length skirt of intertwined snakes. Grisly subject aside, it was a lovely piece, and looked innocuous enough, although he was certain it was anything but.

More sirens wailed outside. Dammit. He knew what he had to do next and he hated it. Pulling out his cell, he punched in a number he'd hoped never to use again. After a moment, General Len Fuller picked up.

"Joshua! Can I hope this is a social call?"

"Wish it was, Len. I think a Company man just took a bullet here in Mexico City."

"What? Where are you?"

"I'm at the Gran Azteca downtown — big archaeological do. A few minutes ago, a guy bumped into me, shoved a bundle into my hands, gasped something about a hand-off and died."

"Died. What do you mean 'died'?"

"As in to be no more. Shot in the back by a sniper. Next target was a security guard who came to help. After that they tried really *really* hard to get me."

"This is not good, Joshua."

"I think I figured that part out for myself, Len. I'm the one who just had the Maltese Falcon experience, remember?"

The general allowed an amused grunt at the reference. "What was in the bundle? Did you look?"

"Of course I looked. It's a small figurine of the Aztec earth goddess Coatlicue. Jade with turquoise insets under the eye sockets."

"A who?"

"Koh-at-lee-kway," he repeated, breaking the name into

distinct syllables for Fuller. "Aztec goddess. Fertility. Earth. All that kind of thing. It's a repro of a larger stone sculpture, but not the one you usually see. You know, the big one with two snakes sprouting from her neck? Anyway, this is modern, only three, maybe four inches high, but still intrinsically valuable because of the materials used." He placed the statuette back onto the desk. "It's pricey, but not valuable enough to shoot anyone over."

Fuller chuckled. "I've missed your on-the-fly evaluations."

"There's more. He knew me."

The general went quiet. Finally he said, "Did you recognize him?"

"Yeah . . . sort of. As I said, I think he was a Company man. . . Riddenour, maybe? I dunno. I met a lot of operatives from a lot of agencies in my active days. Len, the guy knew my name, rank *and* codename."

There was a commotion on Fuller's end. After a moment Katzen heard the General's aide, Colonel Vaughn DeVries' southern drawl. "Josh is right, sir. The CIA just had an op go all pear-shaped in Mexico City. I pulled in some favors and got the details. This here's the sitrep, sir."

Katzen heard shuffling paper, then Fuller came back on the line, "Your memory is better than you think. The agent's name was, indeed, Riddenour. Marcus Riddenour and it was a CIA cock-up. A big one. The Company intercepted a drop — they won't say exactly what from exactly who, but this was the item agent Riddenour had — your coatly. . . ."

"Dingus," Katzen offered.

"Dingus works," the General agreed. "Riddenour was supposed to deliver it to someone at the conference. We don't know who, but it doesn't matter because the shooting screwed that pooch raw. Everyone's security forces are all over the place and you can bet the people Riddenour took the dingus from are in play, too. The CIA have a back-up location ready, though. They're asking for our agent in place to complete the mission."

"Fine. Who's your agent in place? I'll get the piece into their hands and—"

"Josh?" the general interrupted. "*You're* our agent in place."

His insides went cold. His mouth moved, but no words came out.

Fuller continued, "It's a simple drop. All you need to do is get to the International Airport. It's not far from where you are now. There's a big hotel right by terminal two, the AC Aureole. Your man will be sitting in the main lobby at twenty hundred hours tonight. He'll be reading the New York Times and wearing a red shirt — one of those guayabera things. Sit down near him. Tuck the statuette down into the seat cushion in back of you and leave. Don't be late. He'll only stick around for twenty minutes at most."

Katzen said nothing. He still hadn't found his voice. The cold inside was giving way to disbelief.

"Josh? Are you still there? You need to get moving if—"

Disbelief flashed over into anger. "I'm never going to be free, am I?"

"Josh. . . ."

"No matter where I go, what I do or who I become, this shit will always find me, won't it?"

"Josh, calm down."

"*No!* No, I *won't* calm down. Your 'simple drop' already has at least two guys in body bags downstairs. People I don't know are actively trying to kill me. *Again.* I'm out, General! This was supposed to be over."

"I understand, Joshua. It's a lot to ask, but we need you to do this."

Katzen was silent again. His breath came in angry gasps. "Josh? Will you do it?"

"Like I really have a choice. Yes. I'll make your simple fucking drop."

Fuller started to say something else, but Katzen hit the End button and tossed the phone onto the bed. It bounced once, then landed on the other side, against the dresser.

"Moses! I'm tired of this shit."

With any luck, he'd never have to explain this cock-up to Rosenberg. The good doctor took a dimmer view of his friend being dragged back into the spy game than he did himself. Currently, Katzen was angry enough for both of them. Even though it felt like an eternity ago, he'd only just left his friend talking to a group of fellow archaeologists at the convention center. If things followed the usual pattern, they'd talk for at least another hour, then, since it was getting late, likely wander off together for dinner somewhere. Given the time frame, the drop mission would be over and done with well before the archaeologists found their way back home. Need to know was sometimes a good thing. Rosenberg would have a shit-fit when he found out about the shootings, though. That was likely to be the buzz for the duration of the conference. He hoped none of the spectators got a good look at him. That could get dicey.

He checked the time. It was edging onto six o'clock. Correction. Edging onto eighteen hundred hours. If the op was on military time, he might as well get back into thinking that way again — for now, anyway. He sighed and peeked around the drapes. His room was on the opposite side from the original shooting, but no sense in making himself a sitting duck. The sniper got a good look at him through the scope. No way they couldn't have. With the area swarming with officialdom of all flavors, no doubt the shooter was long gone, but it was best not to take chances. He tucked the re-wrapped goddess into his waistband, pulled a fresh dark blue dress shirt down over it and headed out.

Stepping into the hall, the first thing he noticed was that the elevators were getting a workout. It seemed that everyone who had been downstairs when the chaos happened were returning to their rooms at the same time. The stairs were better, anyway. Better to stay out of sight until he *had* to break cover. That brought up another matter. Snagging a cab was an attractive idea, but probably a bad one. Chances were, the people hunting him would have eyes on all the taxi stands in the area and they had him at a disadvantage: they knew what *he* looked like. He needed some distance between himself and the Azteca before even thinking about a cab.

At ground level, he veered away from the main lobby and entered a corridor that led past the pool, the gym and the steam room. Somewhere ahead was an entrance to an arcade mall that linked several of the larger hotels. Earlier in the day, when he and Rosenberg were checking in, the ingrained spy part of his brain had dutifully recorded all diagrams, maps, possible escape routes and exits. Old habits died hard, but sometimes came in useful. According to the colorful map hanging behind the registration desk, if he went through the arcade, he could remain under a roof for several blocks with the exception of a courtyard and one place he'd have to cross at street level.

As he stepped into the hubbub of the arcade, he

became a tourist. He strolled the shops, examined souvenir kitsch, sipped overpriced espresso in the ubiquitous coffee chain store and leafed through colorful brochures touting the wonders of Mexico. He tried on clothing, mostly jackets and hats. Eventually he bought a hat; a dark-colored straw one with a wide brim. He twirled through a rack of sunglasses, but decided against buying any. Daylight was fading outside and, while they might be a decent disguise element, he'd choose being able to see over additional anonymity.

By the time he reached the terminus, he was sure he didn't have a tail. Well, pretty sure. If he was being tag teamed, all bets were off. In the men's room nearest the exit, he tucked his blond ponytail up under the hat and checked the result in the mirror. It would do. It would have to. He didn't have time for more.

Stepping out of the close atmosphere of the arcade, he paused to savor the cooling evening air. It was nice, even if a trifle diesel-scented. He turned toward the nearest taxi stand, but only managed one step before the point of a knife pressed into his back brought him up short. Guess he hadn't been so tailless after all.

The blade nudged him, urging him forward. He obeyed. Walking past the line of cabs, his eyes slid to the reflective windows of the vehicles. The knife-wielder was roughly his height, a little younger and a little heavier. He also seemed to be alone — at least as far as he could tell without turning his head more.

The knife guided him past the taxis and up the street to a narrow alley, then down the alley, through several turns to a garbage-filled cul-de-sac. A hard shove between the shoulder blades pitched him head-long into the trash. He pulled himself up and turned to find the blade inches from his nose. He followed the arm up to a hard face, scarred by life and many knife fights. Katzen was just starting to wonder if he'd walked into a common mugging when the man made the universal motion of "hand it over" and said simply, "Coatlique."

The anger that had smoldered since the phone call with Fuller flared. The dark man saw it happen and a touch of uncertainty entered his eyes.

Katzen picked himself up and snarled, "Get that out of my face!"

The eyes may have flashed momentary doubt, but it was gone now and the blade didn't waver.

"Do you not speak English?" Fury hardened into a white-hot point in the center of his chest. "I can give you that in Spanish. I can give it in Russian — even Urdu if you want. It's all gonna be the same. *Back off.*"

The man understood. He just didn't care. A grin warped the map of scars, then he moved. If Katzen hadn't been expecting it, the blade would have slashed him from scalp to chin. He threw himself backward and brought his legs around, knocking his assailant off balance.

He rolled to his feet and kicked hard, feeling the man's nose crunch under his boot. The knife fell from suddenly unresponsive fingers. Katzen kicked again, but anger made him clumsy. He went wide, giving his opponent the opening to grab his foot and smash him against the wall. In a fluid move, the dark man reclaimed the knife and lunged. Katzen twisted aside, landing an elbow in the man's midsection. Air oofed out. He followed with a double-fisted hammer punch to the side of the scarred man's head. The assailant swayed, stunned. Another blow sent him face down into the pile of trash.

In an instant, Katzen was on him, grabbing a double handful of shirt, pulling him around, fist bunched for another punch — then stopped and let the body slip back onto the rubbish. Even in the dim light of the alleyway, it was obvious the fight was over. The man's own knife protruded from his ribs. Katzen's anger drained away, leaving him limp and slightly shaky.

Katzen straightened his clothing as best he could, regathered his ponytail and re-situated the hat. Making sure the statuette was still secure in his waistband, he walked back the way they'd come. Rather than exiting where they'd entered though, he took the first left and rejoined the flow of passersby a few blocks farther away from the downtown hotels. He saw no one else in the alley and no one on the street gave him as much as a second look. He'd made it another block before he realized the man had tagged him along the ribs at some point. It stung and blood dampened the side of his dark dress shirt.

First garbage, now blood. He'd need a new shirt — and a few other things. There was a bodega across the intersection. Music spilled from its open door and the inside lights made the items within glow against the gathering dusk like the contents of an Aladdin's cave. There were several racks of clothing on the walkway outside the shop. Almost at once, he was drawn to a charcoal gray guayabera shirt with a silvery white floral pattern embroidered on it. Okay, a little flash, and a bit pricey, but he'd had a shitty day and he *liked* it. A little black faux leather butt pack on a shelf just inside had possibilities, too. He reached for it. The slice along his ribs pulled and shot fire through him. *Damn!* He hadn't felt it that badly before. No doubt adrenaline was still pumping through his system, dulling the pain, delaying shock.

Better get what he needed quickly and get the hell out of Dodge before it dissipated. When he crashed, he was going to crash hard.

Dropping the shirt and pouch into a plastic shopping basket, he moved along the aisles to a shelf holding first aid supplies, then stopped, hand hovered over a roll of gauze. The last thing he wanted was for someone be able to ask if an Americano came in hurt. His blond hair made him stand out enough without that making him even more memorable. Nearby was a bin filled with packages of white, cotton handkerchiefs. Beautiful. If he could find tape, those would do nicely. At length, the widest tape he could find in the shop was in a stand-up display featuring a wide-eyed Japanese cartoon cat and her friends. Amid the colorful figurines, coin purses, hair ornaments and cell phone cases were rolls of pink plastic gift-wrapping tape dotted with the happy cat's round, white face. Oh well. There was that old saying about beggars and choosers. At the moment, he was solidly on the beggar side of the equation. He dropped the tape into his basket, picked up a couple more items on a whim and headed for the cashier, an elderly man who hadn't looked up from his racing paper since Katzen had entered.

Farther up the street, an oasis of hotels glowed. They were not quite as upscale as the Azteca, but solidly mid-range. Made to order. He drew a few looks and raised some eyebrows as he crossed the lobby in search of a public restroom. He entered the first one he found. Inside, a man was washing up at the row of sinks. He gave Katzen a suspicious once-over in the mirror. Katzen smiled, nodded pleasantly and made for one of the stalls, hoping the bright florescent lighting didn't make the blood too noticeable against the dark fabric of his ruined dress shirt. He managed to hold back until he heard the man leave, then threw up. Violently.

Later, shaky and spent, he cleaned up at the now-vacant row of sinks and bandaged the long, shallow cut as best he could. When he finished, the pressure bandage he assembled was a little bulkier and stiffer than he liked, but the loose-fitting guayabera covered it well. He buried his old shirt deep in the trash, cinched the butt pack around his waist and headed out. He'd need that taxi now. The adrenaline had drained half-way though his bandaging job. No way he could hoof it all the way to the AC Aureole now.

Incredibly enough, he was running early. Not by a lot, but enough that he wandered for a bit in search of a place to pass the time. It was quite a tour. If the Gran Azteca was upscale, this place was *off* the scale. Soon, he located the main lounge, an airy wood and leather oasis with an amazingly long bar backed by rank upon rank of gleaming bottles. Perfect. A comfortable chair and a splash of scotch would go a long way to help him feel human again.

He took over a small bistro-style table with a view of the room and was savoring his second sip when movement at the entrance caught his eye. A handsome Latina wearing a tightly tailored maroon business suit stepped through. She was followed by two wide, deeply-tanned men who, standing shoulder to shoulder, nearly filled the double doorway of the bar. With their bronzed skin, they looked like a matched pair of metal golems. The woman looked around and, when her eyes lit on Katzen, broke into a wide smile.

"There you are!" she said. "We've been looking all over for you."

Shit.

XX SIW Goes Platinum

When Katzen first entered the lounge, a good-sized group of people had occupied the tables against the windows, but they'd left while he was ordering his drink. Now there was only the bartender, himself and the three newcomers. He didn't like those odds. The woman glided across the hardwood floor and took possession of the seat across from him. Her mountainous companions pulled chairs from nearby tables and took up posts on either side of the tiny table, chairs angled to make leaving difficult.

He set the glass onto the cardboard coaster and treated her to a charming smile. "Looking for *me*? Really? Have we met? Surely I'd remember if we had."

"We were perhaps not formally introduced, but I am familiar with you all the same — with your moves. You are very cool. Very professional, even when the man you have been talking to dies before your eyes."

She's the sniper. It wasn't speculation; it was a certainty. Aloud, he said, "It sounds like I should be flattered."

A few more guests drifted in. Looked like business was picking up again.

"Oh, definitely. I am most impressed," she said. Abruptly, she leaned over the small tabletop bringing her face so close to his, he could see the golden flecks in her brown eyes and smell mint on her breath. "Our man Gregorio contacted us an hour ago saying he'd seen you exiting the arcade mall. We have heard nothing from him since." Her voice dropped to a seductive purr. "You haven't done something . . . unpleasant . . . to our dear Goyo, have you?"

Ah. His knife-wielding dance partner had a name. He took a small comfort in the knowledge that he hadn't missed a tail in the arcade, after all. Gregorio had picked him up as he'd exited. Bad luck, not bad spycraft. The woman's proximity was uncomfortable, but he didn't pull back. That was probably what she wanted; to assert power over him and take complete control of the situation. Instead, he said, "Gregorio. I don't believe I was formally introduced to that gentleman, either. I couldn't venture a guess as to what happened to him."

In the end, it was she who blinked. She sat back, regarding him silently for several long minutes. He calmly finished his scotch and waited for her to speak. At length she said, "Who *are* you?"

He shrugged. "Just a guy enjoying a drink after a long day."

She chuckled. "No. You are CIA. You have obviously been playing this game for a while, given your skill and that you are . . . . What is the American saying? Not a spring rooster?"

"Oh, now you're just being hurtful."

She made a disgusted noise deep in her throat. Waving her hand vaguely in his direction, she said, "Enough small talk. He must have the statuette on him somewhere. Search him."

"Won't that be a bit awkward in such a public venue?" he said, nodding slightly toward the bar. Another group had joined the first and were putting in their orders.

In answer, the golem to his left calmly reached over and gave the leather butt pouch a solid yank. The force popped the cheap plastic clasp open and nearly pulled Katzen onto the floor.

"Wow," he said, re-seating himself and straightening the gray guayabera. "You could have just asked."

Golem #1 ignored him and rooted inside the pouch for a moment before a grin cracked the stony face. The grin grew broader as he withdrew a small, brown paper-wrapped bundle.

"Yes," the woman hissed. "That is it! That is the package the CIA agent gave him this afternoon. Quickly, get it upstairs. We will finish here."

Katzen didn't like the inflection Sniper-Woman put on the word "finish", but other things were demanding his attention. The exit of Golem #1 left that side unprotected. At roughly the same time the thug had exited, a large group of casually-dressed people entered. Some were deeply tanned and some had a bookish quality. He guessed they were participants in the CCSAA. They had the air of people coming back from a good meal, but were still reluctant to call it a night. They chatted, milling about. A splinter broke off and went to the bar, leaving the larger assemblage directly in front of the doorway.

In an instant, Katzen stood and side-stepped into the space recently vacated by Golem #1. Before Sniper-Woman or Golem #2 could react, he was threading his way through the clustered archaeologists and out into the corridor. The last he saw of Sniper-Woman was her fury-contorted face turned toward him before a laughing, drink-clutching group blocked the view.

Stopping in the bathroom made him later than he liked getting to the lobby. He relaxed a little when he caught sight of a largish, bearded man wearing a festive red guayabera in one of the corner chair arrangements, apparently engrossed in an unfolded copy of the New York Times. He knew Sniper-Woman and Golem #2 couldn't be too far away. There really wasn't time to go through the rigamarole the planned drop required. Not if they both wanted to get out with their skins intact. Oh well. He'd never been a stickler for protocol and a white straw hat resting on the table at the reader's elbow gave him an idea.

The lobby was extremely busy, so he didn't have to worry too much about cover as he made his way across. Passing the Times reader, he stumbled, bumping into the side table and knocking the straw hat to the floor.

"Oh, man! I'm *so* sorry!" he said. Bending to retrieve the hat, he murmured. "Heads up. Company's coming." Straightening, he returned the head gear it to its owner, at the same time he dropped the actual statuette, now swathed in a cotton handkerchief that was slightly soiled from having spent the last half hour as part of his compress bandage, into the recesses of the chair.

The Times reader beamed and accepted the hat with a nod of understanding. "No harm done, sir," he said. Katzen barely saw the movement as the package disappeared under the red guayabera.

"Have a good one," he said, then turned and exited, gladly exchanging the bright-lit, air-conditioned lobby for the dimmer lighting of the porte-cochère and humidity of the tropical night.

He snagged a taxi just as a bellman finished off-loading a towering stack of luggage onto a hotel cart. He had no intention of going straight back to his own digs. He'd have to do a little back-tracking before that. They might have some idea he was booked into the Gran Azteca, but they couldn't be sure. Still, he'd need to change his appearance a bit and stay out of sight until the conference ended. A pain in the ass, but probably nothing compared to the one Sniper-Woman was going to have when their boss opened the bundle to discover a small figurine, between three and four inches high, of a wide-eyed Japanese cartoon cat.

The Peace Bringer's Crossing
Andrea Gilbey

"Captain, signal to the vanguard to descend to one thousand atmons and prepare for landing."

"But Lady, this place looks hostile."

The tall woman looked at him squarely, her orange flecked brown eyes firm. He lowered his gaze instinctively, brought up from infancy to avoid looking directly at the Sky-Ruler On Earth, just as one may not look at the Being itself without being blinded.

"And that is why we must land there."

She knew she had no need to say more. The man bowed his head sharply, raised his arms in front of his face in a precise and correct clenched-fisted crossed wrist salute, and bounded athletically up the wooden steps to the wheelhouse of the gondola.

Samarah watched him go and an amused smile flickered across her face. She turned back to the prow of the ship and gripped the rail tightly, noting absently how taut the veins and sinews in the backs of her hands became. Landing was always tense, however many thousand times she had ordered it.

The blare of the horn from the wheelhouse alerted the two lead vessels, and the captain of the foremost ship gave the "We hear" signal with the on-board mirrors.

Flashes above Samarah's head, even brighter than the light surrounding the vessels, transmitted her order to the lead craft and she watched as the burners flared then dimmed in the first canopy, then the second, then recognised the familiar but not unpleasant sinking feeling as the royal gondola started its descent.

Her cousin was back at her side almost silently. From the corner of her eye she could see the muscle in his jaw bulge as he clenched his teeth.

"Captain?"

She tried again in a softer tone, "Pantep?"

"Samarah, one of these missions will be one ocean crossing too far for you, you realise that, don't you?"

She shrugged, "What choice do I have?"

She shielded her eyes with her arm to turn her face up towards the Sky-Ruler.

"You cannot force the whole of creation to follow our ways," Pantep growled impatiently.

She looked at him sideways, and he stared back, risking a royal reprimand.

"I must try," she said calmly.

~*~

The land rising from the icy sea ahead was grey and barren, with a coating of snow on the highest points. From the heart of it rose a slate tower of three concentric baileys, the topmost and centre tower showing sudden metallic flashes at the window ports. Weapons? In any case it seemed that the inhabitants had seen the advancing travellers.

The three vessels descended silently, but although the air around the royal gondola was warm the sea ahead stayed grey and cold, and the protective orb of golden sunlight surrounding the small procession grew smaller and smaller.

Samarah frowned. That shouldn't be happening. The royal fleet's power was having no effect on the atmosphere of this place.

Pantep fidgeted uneasily at her side.

"They must have some kind of . . . invisible wall around this place," he mused.

Samarah laughed, but the laugh sounded unconvincing even to her. She knew why Pantep was even more uptight than usual — in charge of the lead ship was his daughter, Cordavah, on her first mission as captain. Samarah had shown great confidence in her young cousin's abilities by awarding her command of the vanguard.

The lead gondola splashed down into the waves, the crew running around on the flight deck like busy insects to gather up the canopy before it hit the water. A salt water soaked canopy was a lethal problem when combined with the gas and fire needed to inflate it for the homeward journey.

A ramp was being lowered from the rocky island and signs of activity at the opening it revealed suggested that a greeting vessel was being launched. Samarah held out her hand, knowing even before she did so that her captain would have her viewing glass ready. She lined up the sights and adjusted the position of the lenses along the bronze rod. The people climbing into the boat — two, no, three of them, were dressed in baggy grey trews and black long sleeved tunics, with their feet encased in heavy, shapeless boots. She scanned their faces intently for signs of aggression, but the faces looked blank and dull. Maybe that *was* their aggressive expression?

The royal gondola rocked as it hit the water and for few seconds the escort vessel was out of sight behind the waves.

Samarah steadied herself and re-focussed her glass, watching as her young cousin made gracious gestures of introduction and thanks to the greeting party and stepped confidently into the small barge, accompanied by her landing party. The lead vessel sailed out of view behind the rocky land to find a mooring and the second ship glided forward to be met by another escort barge. Samarah straightened her white linen dress and smoothed her hair.

~*~

"Your Excellency, may I present the Lady Samarah," Cordavah intoned slowly and respectfully, her words coming through clouds of icy vapour. She gestured to her older cousin without looking directly at either her or the motionless elderly woman seated on the hard chair in the echoing chamber. The girl's meaning was clear, but the host's translator dutifully interpreted in an expressionless tone of voice.

The seated women spoke in the same toneless manner. The translator bowed, once to his mistress, and again to the visitors, his hands tucked into the opposite sleeves of his tunic.

"Citizen Hallvana welcomes you and asks you your purpose in visiting our community," he droned.

Samarah slid her arms from her unaccustomed warm cloak to make a salute, hurriedly tightened it around her shoulders once more, and spoke directly to the enthroned figure.

"Madam, we are peace bringers. We come from a society that has no war, no violence, no misery, no poverty. For centuries we have travelled to share our peace and light with the world. This is my duty as Sky-Ruler On Earth, and we are here to bring warmth to your country."

XX SIW Goes **Platinum**

The interpreter had moved to stand behind his leader's chair and was murmuring a translation into the woman's ear. The leader's face remained stony.

Samarah continued, "As we approached, we noticed that our light and warmth were unable to affect your climate. Is there. . . ," she hesitated, unsure how to put her question tactfully, "is there some deep sadness in this place?"

As the interpreter spoke Hallvana's attendants took slow steps closer to the throne, as though protecting their leader. Samarah's landing party did not move, but she could feel waves of warmth and happiness emanating from them, pushing gently against their hosts' cold hostility.

The man stood watching his mistress, waiting for her to give him words to translate, but instead Hallvana stood and faced Samarah.

"I speak your language . . . a little," she said with a slight bow. She straightened her back and looked directly into Samarah's face with a stare that held dignity and anger.

"Our lives are not yours to amend. We have lived this way for all time. What right have you to impose your ways on us?"

Something in the back of Samarah's mind itched. Where had she heard those words earlier?

"We bring you nothing but good," she replied, forcing a warm smile through chattering teeth. "Our forebears learned the secret of eternal and boundless peace and happiness and we wish to share it." She held her arms out in a gesture of giving, and immediately regretted it, feeling the cold of the chamber bite at her bones.

Hallvana's face flickered and her body tensed. Anger? No, Samarah realised, this was fear! Fear? Of happiness?

"We cannot change," the old woman said, harshly. "How

can peace and happiness dwell here, in this hard, cold place? You know nothing."

A movement in the corner of her eye distracted Samarah. Cordavah was walking towards one of the grey clad attendants, her arms outstretched, and a smile on her face of utter joy and welcome. Samarah felt a flicker of annoyance. Did the girl not feel the cold? Wait . . . she was cold and becoming angry — the place was starting to affect her.

"We must leave!" she cried, whirling round wide eyed to face Pantep. "This place is dangerous."

Pantep's eyes were fixed on his daughter.

"Wait," he whispered, "watch."

Cordavah approached the young attendant and took her hands.

"You are young, you can change and learn to be happy. Come with us."

The grey-clad girl resisted slightly, then a slow smile spread across her face. Her whole body relaxed and a glow of light appeared around the two girls. A gasp arose from the room.

Hallvana shouted harsh words and the girl pulled her hands sharply out of Cordavah's grasp, slinking back into the shadows.

"We leave, now!" cried Samarah, sweeping towards the door, her brain reeling, trying to process what had just happened.

"Lady," Cordavah ran after her. "Cousin, please, we can't just give up!"

"I said, we leave!" Samarah's voice cracked as her shoes tapped across the stone floor.

Hallvana spoke again and four attendants detached themselves from her retinue and moved towards the door.

Samarah drew herself up to her full regal height, but the attendants held back and motioned the visitors to pass ahead of them out of the room. A farewell escort.

~*~

Samarah watched as Cordavah gave the order to fire the burners and fill the canopy. She still felt cold. She leaned back against the railing of the wheelhouse and folded her arms. She had seen the doubting look in Pantep's eyes when she announced that she would travel back with Cordavah to monitor her command skills and knew that her cousin had seen through her. She also knew that his insistence on rigid protocol would never allow him even to *think* "I told you so" in front of her attendants.

As the gondola rose smoothly into the steadily warmer air she shed her cloak and strolled out onto the sunny main deck. The canopy's bright silk billowed as the hot air lifted it up and away from the cold, forbidding island. She took a deep breath and closed her eyes, allowing the peace and warmth from the Sky-Ruler to re-centre her, and felt her disturbance melt away.

She heard Cordavah's soft footsteps behind her but resisted turning to welcome the girl. What was the matter with her?

Cordavah cleared her throat softly. "Lady? Cousin Samarah? I'm sorry if I overstepped a line. I was wrong."

Samarah turned. Her young cousin was standing with her head bowed, arms in the salute position but pointing downward, the most formal sign of respect and submission.

Samarah glided forward and wrapped her arms around the girl.

"No, you were right, I was wrong. But . . . Cordavah, I'm no longer young, maybe my powers are weakening. I was . . . afraid down there."

Cordavah started to protest, but Samarah hushed her.

"You are my heir and will one day be the Sky-Ruler On Earth. Today you have shown yourself truly worthy, and I . . . I have learned an important lesson. Our mission will continue, it must, but it will be in safe hands without me. I can retire. Perhaps this was a good crossing after all." She pulled back and grinned at her young cousin. "Of course your father won't be happy."

They laughed as the older woman took the girl's hand and led her to the railing to watch their warm, peaceful land come into view once more.

Madcap Midwestern Mythologies
Brett Alan Sanders

Freudian Slips
(with apologies to the poet Mr. Frost)

Two roads converge in a wood, you might say. Two cyclones merged for the split second it took to explode both their lives and all that touched them into utter ruin and devastation. Only to resume each one their course like two bandits hightailing it out of there — Helter-Skelter! Criss-Cross Roads! Happy-Go-Lucky! — for opposite borders. In their wake a path of destruction over a good thousand miles in every direction of almost treeless rolling hills. Cow pasture and corn fields wherever you look, with here and there a patch of forest. From the wide spot in the road me and a smattering of exhausted family lines (intermingled and intermarried for-like-*ever*) call our town.

Village, more like it. Or hamlet. And even them's exaggerating a bit. Given the post office — used to be inside the back door of Aunt Elvie's old farmhouse — 's been closed-up nigh on an eternity. And the general store Aunt Agnes used to run, out of business nigh on half of one. Otherwise ain't nothing more'n a bunch of ramshackle houses, rickety and falling apart these many years. Till you get to the schoolhouse in the next town over. Where all the little ones go. Thataway toward the highway that cuts on up, dividing the county almost in half like two lopsided pieces of a gigantic Valentine-heart jigsaw puzzle.

But I was talking about them two raging cyclones blowing their way through our once-contented little community. And it was bound to happen sooner or later, now's I think of it. Only the occasional outsider ever interwove themself into the near incestuous stew that was our peculiar family shrub. Hardly worthy of the exalted designation of tree, misshapen and cursed like it's turned out to be.

Anyways, it come about because of Miss Jocelyn who went traipsing off to foreign places with some comely passerby. Whatchamacallum, let's just say. Even she didn't know his name for absolute sure. When she come back she didn't say nothing about him and no one asked. Before long she just up and married the old preacher man who held church right out of his barn. Every Sunday for the modest assortment of us the spirit happened to be working on at the moment. Still doing it up to the fateful day that I, Maddie S. Polk, village fabulist and yarn-spinner extraordinaire, am fixing to tell you of, honest to gods. Feels like only yesterday, if it were a million years, when they hauled him off to the state penitentiary.

Way Grammy tells it, anyways (over yonder at the asylum where she's been vegetating more years than I've been alive), might as well of all happened yesterday. Some generation or so since Jocelyn's homecoming, here come this other stranger right under the half-blind old preacher's nose. And swept that old girl plumb off her feet, just like the other one swung her all that time before. Looked just like him too, or so I hear. Faster'n you can say Rumplestiltskin, anyways, they was bedded down in the hay up on the barn loft, naked as the day their mommas popped them out.

After the loving, like they say, she was a-sighing and caressing on his back. She's noticing some little bit of a bump on that immense masculine terrain. Some sort of birthmark, an irregular and possibly cancerous growth, a mole or something, as she saw when she finally took a gander. And it looked kind of familiar, she thought. Like something once glimpsed in a dream. Then before you know it they's both runnin around the barnyard, stark naked and screaming bloody murder over the accident of their unwitting transgressive souls. Running past the old cuckold himself who was out on the back porch cleaning his fully-automatic deer-hunting rifle.

Preacher man went blazing mad, then, started shooting right and left. Seeing visions of Heaven and Hell, to hear him tell it, while ranging reckless through a powerful big stretch of farmland. When the dust cleared there wasn't nothing left untouched. Hardly an acre not streaming in savage, screaming blood.

Jocelyn and her erstwhile lover dodged the fire that was exploding behind them from her husband's gun. They say Loverboy's corpse washed up along the river some time later, half eaten by its humungous, mutant catfish. And the madwoman who'd just hooked up with him, though there's other versions that tell it different (slanderous, Gramma Josie insists, against her own otherwise unimpeachable reputation), that raving lunatic who'd just seduced him wound up hung by the neck like laundry from a tree. Hanging there by the abandoned slip of a dress either she or someone else strung her up by.

The handsome foreigner's name, let it be said at last, was just like his own daddy's. The same one who come through that way those several ages earlier. That name being: *Eddie Pussopolous* — Junior, in this case — or something like that.

Grammy's sure now she's remembering it a-right. Says it has some kind of occult or exotic meaning, too.

But that's all Greek to me.

A Secret Place

Bonnie Abraham

A place to withdraw to when you feel rejected — a place to go when you are hurting. But a secret place can keep out healing as well as hurt. There is a time to withdraw into a secret place and a time to go forth — just as there is a time to love and a time to hate — a time to live and a time to die.

A time to die. Death. The ultimate secret place. No one can betray you there — or can they? What if there really is a life after death? What if there really is Someone you are accountable to? What if a person dies, thinking he has escaped it all, and finds he is very, very wrong?

~*~

Judas studied the loop of rope in his hands for only a moment, then slipped it over his head and jumped. The ultimate secret place.

He did a good job of it. He was dead almost instantly.

He heard laughing. Blood-chilling-cold laughing. He looked for the source, but nothing but empty darkness met his eyes. He lifted his hand to his face, or thought he did, but he couldn't feel his hand, couldn't feel his arm moving, couldn't feel his nose. Nothingness.

"Do I have a body?" he wondered. But he could hear the snickering. He couldn't shut it out. "So, I must have ears." The laughing grew louder.

"Welcome to my world," came a thought into his mind. It was not his own thought.

"Where are you?" He asked this aloud in spite of the sure feeling that his thoughts were all he needed to communicate. But he didn't hear his own voice.

"Anywhere. Wherever. Nowhere — take your pick."

"Where am I? I did die, didn't I?"

The laughter echoed loudly inside his head. "Oh, indeed. A splendid job. One you will LIVE to regret for a *loooong* time. It was delicious. You believed it all." The laughter continued to rumble menacingly.

"I don't understand. What did I believe?"

"All of it. Every delusion we threw at you — that you were *sent* to betray Him — that His plan depended on *your* manipulating events so that He took His kingdom by force — that He wouldn't let Himself be crucified — *That He couldn't do it without you.*"

Judas tried to swallow past the dryness in his throat. "Why did He? Why did He allow himself to be arrested? Why didn't He come down off that cross? Why didn't He rain fire down on the Romans?"

"See, you still believe it. Oh, you are a sweet, succulent morsel," gloated the other voice in his head. "I have even told you it was all lies and still you believe."

"He could have driven out the Romans! He could have been king of the whole world! Who could have stopped Him?"

"He is as dead as you. Remember? What do you think? You have *always* trusted your own reasoning power. Surely, you won't abandon it now, just because you are dead, just because you made one small error in your logic."

"Who are you?"

"Oh, you *know* who I am. You and I have been companions for a long time. You remember." The voice changed slightly, to one he had heard before — one he had heard when he was *alive*. "He's telling you His plan. He knows you understand His code. He's letting you know how to make it all happen. He's relying on you." The voice changed back again. "You really *are* stupid, you know. In spite of all the real evidence, you chose to believe *me*, the one who told you what you *wanted* to be true. And you made what He *really* said come true — all by yourself."

"Everyone is saying I betrayed Him. But He betrayed *me*! He *DIED!* And where did that leave me? With nothing! Nothing but death! At least I got to choose the method. No long torturous suffocation on a Roman cross."

The rumble of laughter again. "You think *physical death* is all you needed to worry about? Oh, that is rich."

He didn't know how long the silence lasted before the voice was speaking inside his head again. "You know that He rose again."

"He did what!? Who are you?"

"Haven't you guessed, yet? Oh, better and better! But I won't tell you. You have all eternity to figure it out."

"All eternity?" A dreadful realization came to Judas with those two words. All eternity to remember he had not been betrayed — that he had, in fact, betrayed Messiah. All eternity in this black nothingness with this horrible taunting voice.

"You can, of course, go back and choose again," said the voice, soothingly.

"What do you mean?"

"Just that. You can choose to go back — take your chances with the other One. You'd have to give yourself to

Him totally, of course — let Him do what He wants with you. You'd have to *depend* on Him. You decide."

In the echoing silence that followed, Judas considered. The voice didn't seem to be in any hurry for an answer. Time didn't even seem to exist here. He remembered the awful pain of the rope tightening around his neck until his neck snapped. Had it really hurt that much — taken that long? If he went back, he would never heal completely, he reasoned. *He — the other One —* would heal him enough to keep him alive and useful to Himself. "Isn't that what I would do to someone who betrayed me?" He pictured himself totally dependent on others to bathe him, carry him, feed him. There would be constant pain. *And he would always be the betrayer. Always in debt to* Him.

"No," he said stubbornly, "I won't go back to that. I won't be used. I won't be dependent on someone else!"

"Your will be done." And he heard the laughter again, echoing inside him. "All eternity," cooed the voice. "You are mine for all eternity. Oh, a *tasty* morsel."

Brotherhood of Man and Beast

Brett Alan Sanders

"Volvieron a sus bestias, y a ser bestias ..."
(They returned to their beasts and to being beasts ...)
– Miguel de Cervantes, *Don Quixote*

Mr. Evolution, as John Doherty soon came to be known in that rural Indiana county, had been aware that he was in uncharted waters when he thought to bring the actual writings of that old heretic of monkey-science, Darwin, into what he preferred to think of as his humanities curriculum. The course in question was simply sophomore English, though there were no electives, and so he felt justified in taking certain liberties toward broadening his students' horizons.

His aim was at once civic and rhetorical, in the sense that he wanted his students to be, not mere voters in periodic local and national elections, but (infinitely more vital, he thought) informed and active participants in a national civic dialogue that the political classes would only be dragged into kicking and screaming. And this in the era of climate-change denial and, in neighboring Kentucky, a museum of Creationist science, a century and a half after the *Origin of Species* first appeared in 1859.

Clearly, as the community had sized Doherty up by the end of his first semester at that school, he was an idealist and an eccentric whose aspirations were no better appreciated than understood.

Not quite a handful of years after that first semester, he was about to find himself embroiled in his first bona fide controversy when the cute little redhead in his second-period class went home and reported to her preacher-man grandfather what they were up to in that ungodly classroom.

"He says," she averred, with naive good will but somewhat less than precise accuracy, "that we're all descended from a pack of chimpanzees."

No, Doherty would later clarify; not exactly, he explained, in the context of the crucial fourth chapter of the *Origin of Species*, with its concept of natural selection in the evolutionary cycles of the lower animals and other life forms; the idea was not that we come from them, but only that we and our cousin primates all descend along different lines from a common ape-like ancestor: that most frightful of evolutionary concepts that Darwin himself kept under wraps until, twelve years after the publication of the *Origin*, he published (in 1871) *The Descent of Man*.

"But I don't see the difference," she complained to the reverend grandfather. "We come from an ape or an ape's ancestor? Don't it amount to the same thing either way?"

"You're absolutely right," he assured his pride and joy, "it's a distinction that's always struck me as so much intellectualized anti-prophetic fine-poin-*TIF*-icating, if you ask me."

Just a bait and a trickery, he might have added, to bring man and woman down from the true genealogy of angels and children of God where their place really lies.

"Remember, like the Good Book says, you're just a wee bit lower than the angels, and don't your pretty little head forget it."

He reached forward, meanwhile, to scratch the shaggy

ears of the ailing old Sheltie looking tiredly up at him from where, close between arthritic paws, her head touched the rug.

"Which puts us on a whole different plane than our friends the animals whose guardians and protectors we nevertheless remain."

~*~

It was on the morning after the evening of the girl's first complaint that her grandfather marched into the school and confronted the teacher outside his classroom door.

"I'm the Reverend Jonas Paul Harris," he said. "Just come from talking to both principal and superintendent."

He spoke loudly, in something approaching the rising crescendo of voice that punctuated his Sunday sermons. His reddening forehead and face shone forth like brimstone from snow-white hair.

"Told them I don't cotton to no preaching of diabolical Darwinism to the captive and impressionable youth of this God-fearing community! Let alone in a class that's got nothing to do with the physical sciences, so-called!"

He drew himself up with the dignity of Christian scholar and prophet at once, his lips slightly upturned now in an inward laugh at how he'd gotten the teacher's back up, like some coal-black tomcat at midnight on Halloween. He proceeded with a clearing of throat and a slightly less abrasive tone.

"At least teach it alongside Bunyan and Milton, why don't you, if you want to give a fairer perspective. Anyhow, I'm not the kind of man myself what just unleashes his assault on the helpless and unwitting, with no hint of Christian warning. So let this serve for notice that, come Monday next, I'll be addressing the school board."

So on that Monday, after calming as best he could the public-relations sensibilities of both principal and superintendent, emailing each of them his detailed if still unpolished unit plans, inviting them then to witness for themselves what it was he was really up to, on that Monday the almost blind-sided teacher was prepared to present his case for academic freedom — and for the necessary rigors of a broad liberal-arts and science-based education at the dawning of the twenty-first century.

His intentions, he told the board, were not to usurp the power of the pulpit or even to challenge it, but simply to seize legitimate academic ground to which the pulpit had no rightful claim, to work across curricula to present an ill-understood and misrepresented scientific principle that had already borne rich fruit across scientific fields and the full range of the humanities. Including literature and the rhetorical arts of persuasion, shared intellectual inquiry, and spirited dialogue about real and demonstrable problems we face as a nation and world. None of which we have the slightest hope of fixing while embroiled in uncivil cold war over religious and moral disputations, un-resolvable by any array of objective or subjective evidence alone.

In any case, given how little space the most productive of all biological theories actually garners in the average high-school biology text, and how much time that equates to in the average biology course, and how under-appreciated Darwin remains as the master of civil, fair-minded reasoning and explication that he was, call him what they will, but this upstart of a teacher felt more than justified in bringing some of that accessible and eloquent writing back to the table where it rightly belonged.

"And with it — though not *Pilgrim's Progress* or

Paradise Lost that the good Reverend suggests; I fear they would hopelessly bore the kids! — I'm working in a variety of other sources that will help put the question in its widest possible context, and give students more than adequate practice at decoding, interpretation, and synthesis of texts and media."

"Will you give equal time to Creation science?" one of the preacher's confederates shouted from the audience.

"No, ma'am, I will not treat anyone's pseudo-science as being on anything near the evidential footing of Darwinian theory. Though we will do our best to examine the debate in its historical, political, and religious context."

Yet by meeting's end, at which the Board took no decisive action one way or the other, Mr. Evolution and his reverend adversary were hand-shaking and back-slapping as they discussed how the two of them might still collaborate in the interest of the children's well-rounded exposure to an ever-expanding universe of ideas. The details remained inchoate, incipient, but the intention was sealed by a handshake. As a gentlemen's bargain, it seemed assured.

~*~

On the Sunday following that school board meeting, they were just sitting down to the grandmother's home cooking. That both men were gathered at the same table at all might seem, if not outright miracle, a singular and precariously hopeful experiment in the reconciliation of rivals. But seated at that table they were. Mr. Doherty and his girlfriend at the home of the Reverend Mr. Harris, his wife, and that cute little redhead in Doherty's class: the Reverend and Mrs. Harris's granddaughter and ward.

"Esther, you should o' seen and heard it," Grandpa declaimed.

All were seated at that great oak table except for grandma and granddaughter, who were bringing the last of the fixings to set upon it.

"I have to give it to you again, teacher-man. You didn't turn tail like I thought you would under the barrage of my eloquence and the supporting noise of my concerned parishioners."

Becca smiled as she sat down across from her teacher's pretty fiancée, who smiled back at her and made a point of repressing a conspiratorial giggle at the hyperbolic banter of these men.

"You came out guns a-blazing, stood your ground there like a man, and so won my grudging respect."

"*Vini, vidi, vici,*" the younger man answered, mischievously grinning and audaciously quoting Caesar, blowing off the smoke from a pair of imaginary pistols.

His conversant laughed boisterously. The dog, from the carpet just off the dining area, lifted her head for a moment before laying it down and drifting back to sleep.

"You came and you saw, I'll give you that, boy! But until I surrender, you ain't conquered! And let me tell you, I don't give up easy!"

The plates were soon filled with Southern-style fried chicken with mashed potatoes and thick brown gravy, with made-from-scratch biscuits, with corn and green beans and carrots from the family garden that had been canned in the summer for winter eating. It was still February, but there had been precious little snow and a cold that was just wet and dreary. Conversation turned to the not-too-blushing bride and a planned June wedding. The old preacher cleared his throat and directed his attention her way.

"Tell me, Susan, do you believe in God?"

"I do, yes."

"You go to church?"

"I'm a faithful and practicing Methodist, Reverend."

"And this man you think to marry? Do you know whether he believes in God?"

She turned to her fiancé and smiled, winked at him.

"I think you'd have to ask John that question yourself."

"So do you?"

"Do I believe," he echoed. Returning the questioner's sharp baiting gaze, a flash of challenge in his own eyes. "I guess I'd have to declare myself agnostic on that question."

"By which you mean atheist!"

"No. I just think God's existence a distinct unlikelihood, something—"

"You don't believe it, in the existence of God and the Resurrection!"

"—something I don't know anything about."

"You don't believe, that makes you an atheist! A sorry heathen!"

"Now, dear," his long-suffering Esther interrupted, "don't be so contentious and ornery."

The old Sheltie dog in the other room painfully stood up, slowly, perked her ears in the direction of the noise; while Susan, a biologist with the forest service, though her natural inclination was to avoid this pointless argument altogether, decided she should at least say a tactful word or two on her entrapped partner's behalf.

"You know, Reverend Harris, while I do believe in God, I also know that John's a good, decent man. And I know many Christians, besides me, who also accept Darwinian theory."

The good Reverend, who could well appreciate this

young woman's Christian desire to "stand by her man," as the country singer put it, did not know what else to say without calling her a heathen, too.

"Just saying," she told the ensuing silence. "I don't mean to offend."

After a short pause, deciding to pretend she had said nothing, the Reverend pounded his fist on the table like some future judgment-day gavel, pointing a finger back at the real object of his wrath, then returned to shouting at him.

"Well, by God, then, if you don't believe it, I'll prove you He does! For I know that my Redeemer lives! See if I don't! How dare you, if you can't even acknowledge the Creator of all things? How dare you even think you can teach our children to be moral citizens, capable of harnessing the will of the American people to solve the gravest problems of our sin-stained republic!"

Susan took her fiancé's hand and whispered calming noises. His back was up at the irritation of being dragged here on the false pretense of a friendly meal and discussion and then set upon like the enemy of all things holy and sacred. He looked at his plate and took several deep breaths but even then could not hold his tongue.

"You've heard, perhaps, of this little provision that the Founders put in our Constitution? The same Constitution about whose sacredness and Originalist intentions you fundamentalist zealots are always going on about?"

"You hear that, Esther? He's done gone and used the F-word!"

"It's called the separation of Church and State, and—"

"The F-word, Esther, the one those damn unbelieving liberals are always throwing at us sore-afflicted Christians, in brazen scorn and ridicule!"

"—and believe it or not, it was put there to protect the religious from each other, not just liberal heathens like me from them, so—"

"There he goes again," the preacher shouted, standing by now on both feet and gesticulating like an exorcist in front of Satan's spawn, "there he goes, distorting the words of all that's good and decent!"

"—so you won't have to run off like some latter-day Pilgrims to start some splinter-group, theocratic, witch-hunting, Christian-Talibanish colony on the deserts of Mars!"

Our inflamed teacher, on his feet now, too, slammed a cloth napkin down on his place in a gesture of offended leave-taking.

"That's how I dare teach your children what might not always fit with your fairy-tale sweet Sunday-school lessons! And with that, my girl and I are out of here!"

Later at home, where they lay in bed after the teacher had worked out his own aggression in wanton, calming horseplay, the late afternoon sunlight flowing in through the slats of Venetian blinds, she laughed at him and made mock-angry noises like the almost hairless-bodied ape he had seemed to become.

"Lord, what fools these mortals be," he answered puckishly, between his own laughter and hers.

"Enamored of an ass," she echoed. "Every straight woman's sorry fate."

~*~

At school the morning after that debacle at the dining table, John Doherty looked up at his antagonist who threw on his desk a stack of papers secured by an oversized paper clip. The preacher had spent the last hour in the teacher's lounge copying whole chapters from William Paley's

Natural Theology, that predecessor to Darwinian science from which the latest and best Creationist science was almost wholly derived, without a single significant advance in more than two centuries.

"Here. This is your homework. Next Sunday we review. After a peaceful meal, my Esther commands, with not a blessèd stitch of cantankerous disputations. You choose the next reading."

He turned and went out the door without another word or waiting for a reply. The teacher of evolutionary rhetoric was left shaking his head at the humble brazenness of his friendly antagonist's latest act, and contemplating the inelegant crabwalk of an apology that he himself would offer, at that next meeting, for his own intemperate response.

"And what say you," the preacher asked when the moment was finally arrived, sitting down in the living room for serious conversation, "what say you of Paley's analogy of the watch with its intelligent designer? And of the human eye with its divine Creator?"

"I say that it is indeed elegant. I'll give you that, Reverend."

Preacher Jonas, beaming at this small victory of his, sat upright in an old-fashioned chair with wicker seat and tall wicker back and big solid arms, stroking the ancient Sheltie that Becca had just placed on his lap.

"I remember reading excerpts of it in other texts, but only the original conveys its full impact. Sort of like Darwin's own texts, I suppose, which everyone talks about but few these days have bothered to consult."

"Paley was right, I would like to think, when he said that 'the examination of the eye was a cure for atheism.' What more proof do you need, professor? How could such perfection and foresight be shaped by any other than an intelligent Designer?"

"The proof, so-called—"

The young teacher's eyes flashed, lips curled in an incipient smile. The preacher harrumphed at that arch imitation of his own rustic speech.

"So-called, my sassy boy? You mock me again with your so-called scientific verities?"

"—that proof, so-called, or what you and the good Reverend Paley count as proof, is grounded in shared assumptions based in your common religious hope, secured by an analogy wrapped inside a syllogism."

"The watch and the eye! Elegant, you said! Miraculous!"

"'All complex mechanisms require the intervention of an intelligent designer. The human eye is a complex mechanism. Hence, the human eye requires the intervention of an intelligent Designer.'"

"And what's wrong with that? Chew on these words! Miraculous! Elegant!"

"Elegant within the realm of an invented system of reasoning and logic, a human construct which looks pretty on paper and pretends to prove more than it can. But how does it fare when someone like Darwin wanders outside its artificial limits and imagines a whole new paradigm? 'How stupid of me not to have thought of that,' Huxley said when he first heard Darwin's new theory."

The main difference, John Doherty declared, what makes Darwin's texts more than novelties of exquisite but antiquated thought, (though Paley's did rely on a good amount of detailed observation of the physical world), is the immense array of rock-solid rather than loose and un-rigorous evidence that he brought to bear on his subject — evidence garnered patiently over years of labor and from around the globe — and that Paley could not. Because Paley's central thesis, unlike Darwin's, would not yield to the probing of scientific process.

The Reverend J. P. Harris rubbed his eyes and sighed, drawing a deep breath.

"But I can't agree with you. His evidence and logic are impeccable."

"But that's my point. The logic is fine, the premise mistaken."

The old man shook his head, marveling that this seemingly bright human being could not grasp the truth that stared him in the face.

"So you say, my affectionate foolish humanist. But I have to insist that spiritual tests are their own way of knowing, and they are not to be made light of. There are things, dear friend, that your philosophy cannot explain."

For a while the men fell silent. The women came in and sat down with them. The dog on the old man's lap began to cough and then to whimper.

"Poor Maggie," Becca said. "I wish she wouldn't suffer so."

The preacher caressed the dog tenderly and spoke to her in the tones of a mother comforting an infant. Her breathing grew gradually steadier and her eyes closed in a fitful sleep. They who attended her fell into subdued conversation about the failing health of that beloved pet, about her long history among them and the mileposts of that relationship between man and beast.

"I suppose," the preacher said, "you're gonna have to show your class that old movie *Inherit the Wind*?"

"I hadn't thought of it, though it might not be a bad idea for a culminating activity."

First, there would be what remained of the immediate Darwin unit itself; afterwards, the transition to research and to the informative and persuasive projects and compositions that follow.

"That's where I'm heading, anyway. I want them to apply the rhetorical principles we're studying in the investigation and reporting of their own enthusiasms."

The old man laughed and returned his attention for a moment to petting the dog.

"You do know, of course, that the whole movie's a bunch of bunk and balderdash. It didn't happen the way it's depicted at all, and it makes of one of our unsung populist heroes and national treasures something of a clown. And William Jennings Bryan was no clown and deserved no such dishonor."

"I supposed the play was fictionalized to some extent, but I thought it was basically true to form. As for Bryan, I don't really know much about him except as there revealed."

"Which is to say you know nothing!"

"I accept your rebuke."

And so the preacher explained that Bryan was no benighted religious fanatic and not even quite the Biblical literalist he is made out to have been. He was a common man from the Midwest who, gifted in the arts of eloquence and oratory, struggled against the interests of the rich and powerful who are forever grinding on the face of the poor working man, as Old Testament prophets might have put it. The young upstart atheist teacher might be surprised to know that the three-time Presidential candidate was an opponent of American imperialism in the Philippines, champion of women's rights, and enemy of the gold standard who most famously said: "You shall not press down upon the brow of labor this crown of thorns. You shall not crucify mankind upon a cross of gold."

"He opposed the teaching of evolution in the classroom," the preacher said, "not because he was afraid of science but because he knew how evolutionary theory was giving ground to the enemies of the poor and downtrodden who thought they should just be exploited or let to die off. All on the basis of 'nature red in tooth and claw' — 'survival of the fittest' — with the fittest, naturally, being those with all the hoarded wealth and political power."

"That was Social Darwinism, you know, Herbert Spencer's distortion of Darwin's theory. But, so maybe you want to prep my class for the monkey-trial film when we get to it?"

~*~

In the following weeks, the Darwin unit proper inched toward its natural conclusion and the time approached for the reverend grandfather's presentation to Mr. Evolution's two sophomore classes. Before that, with the teacher's permission, he observed his granddaughter's class again during the culminating discussion on the diabolical book he had hoped to scare off of the curriculum.

John Doherty, on that occasion, recited the famous last sentence of Darwin's most defining volume.

"There is grandeur in this view of life with its several powers, having originally been breathed into a few forms or into one; and that, whilst this planet has gone cycling on according to the fixed law of gravity, from so simple a beginning endless forms most beautiful and most wonderful have been, and are being, evolved."

The citation was projected behind him, but he had it by memory, declaimed with the intonations of an actor on life's stage, Shakespearean soliloquy in the mouth of the heretic evolutionist himself. John fell silent for a moment and let the words sink in. Then he guided the class, by means of a call and response to that statement, on a whirlwind review of the evolutionary thesis from start to finish.

"So what does he mean by those words?"

"Perhaps," spoke a perky brunette, "he wanted to soothe over hard feelings with the church people he knew didn't buy into his theory."

"I do think that makes some sense, Lisa, but was it so much to mend hurt feelings or something else? Did he expect, for instance, that the stodgy old guard of the religious or, more to the point, scientific establishment was going to throw up its arms and say, 'You got it right, Charlie, by gosh! What were we thinking!'?"

"All I know," said a devout or just contrarian farm boy, "is that the devil made him write it, because it's all a bunch of gosh-darn atheist horseshit."

"Thanks for that malodorous thought, but now state your evidence, my friend, or you just struck out."

A wild-haired slacker with a bent for poetry spoke up then in defense of the school's heathen and atheist complement, of which he was a determined representative.

"He *has* no evidence, don't you see? It's like he's afraid to imagine humans as anything but the reason for all existence. Like there's some supernatural busybody up there who really gives a crap whether it's us come out on top or some glorified monkeys like on *Planet of the Apes*."

"But let's not put down anyone's religious beliefs. Enough of the digging into corners and trading insults. And there's no need to pose science and religion as mortal enemies. It's just that, as Stephen Jay Gould put it, science has more to say about physical proofs, and religion more about moral or ethical principles. Just cite your evidence, anyway, and make your point. The best argument wins, not the loudest or snarkiest."

Preacher Jonas, at the end of that rainy weekend, was back again with a four-page front-and-back litany of distortions in the anti-Christian diatribe that was that fanciful work of theater and film called *Inherit the Wind*.

No, he said, that Tennessee teacher wasn't put in jail and didn't face a moment's persecution. Bunch of malarkey! Clarence Darrow didn't get a mob's welcome — balderdash! — he was treated like the celebrity prince he thought he was. Bryan didn't fall down, in a rage over Darrow's bullying him on a question of the earth's age in billions of years or millennia, and die of apoplexy on the courtroom floor — absolute hogwash! — he died a week later at a church dinner after suffering a heart attack.

And the litany went on. Even the atheist poet's jaw dropped as he seemed to hang on every word of that blustery speech. And the preacher didn't once have to glance down at a remaining copy of the paper he had handed out.

~*~

The flowery springtime seemed to dance along. Dogwoods and redbuds bloomed and students agonized over written and oral presentations on their variety of chosen topics. The teacher and his fiancée continued to join the preacher-man's family for Sunday dinners. Once, they turned the tables and invited the good Reverend and his wife and young charge for a meal at their house in town. The Sheltie dog continued her decline and was cared for and made comfortable as much as humanly possible. Teacher John took another risk at controversy when he let one of his stoner kids write his paper and film his presentation in favor of the legalization of marijuana. The stipulations were that he use responsible sources (to which the teacher helped direct him) and that no real marijuana be consumed in any form or shown on the video the class would be watching and evaluating for its strengths of argument and delivery. The preacher's and his Esther's blossoming granddaughter was also a late addition to the bridal party of her teacher's wedding which would take place the weekend after graduation in a joint Methodist and Baptist ceremony at Preacher Jonas's chapel.

"So I still can't persuade you about the intelligent Designer behind the miracle of Creation?" he asked his skeptical young conversant, that paradoxically moral (at least ethically-minded) yet nonbelieving interlocutor, on a Sunday afternoon in May.

They were gathered around the table after the food had been cleared away and they had finished their dessert, looking now at the teacher's illustrated edition of *The Expression of the Emotions in Man and Animals*.

"Not for lack of trying, my good sir, but for goodness sake don't give up."

"Where there's life, there's hope," Susan said. "At least that's what I remember Grover Monster used to say on *Sesame Street*."

"Where there's life, there's hope. That's true enough, isn't it, Esther?"

"But keep in mind that there's always the contrary hope that I might convert you, my dear Reverend, to the eternal verities of Darwinism."

"Bah! A snowball in Hell's chance of that."

Becca, turning a page and looking at one of the illustrations, broke out in a grin and an expressive *aaahhhh!*

"Look, Grandpa Jonas, at the grin on that doggie's face as it nestles up to its human. Don't it make you think of Maggie?"

The Sheltie dog was lying on the floor in a corner by herself. She seemed scarcely to be breathing. Redheaded Rebecca danced over to pet her.

"So even the emotions of this curious brotherhood of man and beast are products of evolution, you want me to believe? Don't we have, in your philosophy, anything that's just ours? That just is? That we get to choose to hold dear and believe in and be comforted by?"

Just then the granddaughter cried out and the Reverend and his wife came running. John Doherty and his bride followed. The dog was convulsing and the girl herself reduced to sobs.

Grandpa reached into a pocket and pulled out a small vial of olive oil that he had consecrated for the healing of the sick.

"Now, the brethren would tell me not to do this, that it's not for the beasts of the field, but this is family, I say, and we're gonna pray this good friend into the fields Beyond, where she'll await us in perfect peace and health."

He knelt down by his Maggie and spilled a bit of oil on her forehead. She continued to tremble, violently. He rubbed the oil in and closed his eyes. The girl and her grandma closed theirs too and folded their arms, both of them weeping, the girl holding on as if she would enwrap herself entirely in the blanket of her wounded compassion.

"We love you, Maggie. You're the best dog ever barked up a squirrel or chased a rabbit."

Susan prayed, too, her modest Methodist prayer, whispering through silent lips. Her lover and best friend, startled skeptic, watched with wide eyes and trembled briefly in his noncommittal way.

The Reverend prayed, tears all down his face but speaking with slow precision, nonetheless.

"God, our Creator and Lord of all things breathing on this earth or swimming in its oceans or rivers or ponds or flying through the sky below Heaven, Father God, in the name of Christ Jesus our Redeemer I ask you to release this good animal from her suffering and let her rest from her labors in peace forever and ever, amen. Bless her and keep her for us, O God, for we already miss her and our hearts are a-breaking."

In the instant he opened his eyes, or so it seemed to those present, those who believed in the grace of God and he who didn't, the Sheltie dog ceased to tremble and lapsed gently into her mortal death.

The preacher and his months'-long interlocutor took turns turning over ground out back of the house under a towering pine. The girl, not quite done crying, carried Maggie to that resting place and laid her down on the pine needles and grass. Her grandfather wrapped the dog in her favorite blanket and eased her into that grave. When they were done praying, they covered her with dirt and went inside. The guests, wordless, hugged their friends and took their leave. The family stayed behind and began the hard work of comforting each other with happy tales of canine love.

Preacher Jonas, as he prepared himself for bed just a few hours later, felt a new stirring inside as he considered that perhaps it wasn't such an unmitigated evil if he did happen, through some wrinkle in God's incomprehensible Plan, to be related to that pack of chimpanzees — though he rather felt more affection for the dog species.

Teacher John, for his part, sat down at home to his school papers. *But the dog was in its death throes anyway,* he thought. *The prayer and its aftermath don't prove anything.* And yet it did occur to him that evening, for perhaps the first time in his adult memory, and more than once then before closing his own eyes to sleep, how comforting it might be for a man of humanistic faith and science to yield his heart, now and then, to the ineluctable mysteries of pure religious or mythological imagination. He kissed his sleeping Susan and thought about attending Methodist service with her some other week.

She's In The Jailhouse Now
Ginny Fleming

We lived in a quiet, picturesque neighborhood with well-groomed lawns — in fact, as I recall, our closest neighbors were the Cleavers.

. . . Okay. In my dreams. Actually, I grew up on a dead-end street in a massive *very* creepy and totally haunted house. There were only four homeowners in the whole neighborhood including my family — the rest of the block being filled with mostly-nice low-income renters. "Mostly-nice" because there were a handful of renters who made their living in a "questionable manner". To put it in PC terms: One could have one's heart's desire on Second Street — if one's heart's desire were guns, knives, drugs or skanky sex.

But still, Second Street in that nostalgic era was a bucolic "Mayberry community". Being a dead-end, all the neighborhood kids played in the middle of the street. Kick ball, Hop-Scotch, marbles, ride our bikes . . . One could buy a snow-cone from my next door neighbor, the neighborhood pedophile: Mr. Diddlephulf. Anything was fair game as long as the "toy in play" didn't land in the open sewer/gutter. Ahhh . . .Hot summer was always a blissful and fragrant time. Yeah . . . it was a Cleaver kind of neighborhood — just two blocks from the police station. I'll repeat that last part: *Just two blocks from the police station.* It figures into this bit of nostalgia — take notes.

On any given day, any given kid would be playing in front of any given house. I take pride that "Our Gang" often landed in my front yard for Kool-Aid and cookies. Mom and Dad both loved kids — *especially*, other peoples' kids . . . (*Whaaaaa?*). On one such day, Mom was digging in her front yard flower garden, minding her own business (a rare occurrence). Suddenly, she raised her head from her dirtly task. A ruckus in the middle of the street. Li'l . . . Bobby . . . Billy . . . Dudley . . . Li'l Snotty-What's-His-Name (quite possibly the most *humungous* eight-year-old in existence) was in my face about some infraction or faux pas. As I remember, he was just a bit livid.

I also remember, I might possibly have been the instigator for this conflict — having lobbed a hefty rock at Li'l Snotty — which, my freaky Olympic-worthy aim being true — met its target upon his lumpy head. In my defense, I can only say . . . I threw pretty good for a girl. An undersized one at that.

Failing to witness my geologic Shot-Put throw, Mom was willing to let it go and allow me to fight my own battles (no Grendel's Mom, she). But then . . . she saw Li'l Snotty turn to his tiny-tiny sister, many years his junior. For absolutely no reason, he pummeled the tot, hitting her hard in the stomach. Mom turned feral tiger and ran into the fray, righteous Sunday School Teacher guns blazing.

I'm sure Mom first tried reasoning with the charming bully-boy, bringing Jesus into the discussion whether He wanted to be there or not. I don't remember any of her come-to-Jesus mini-sermon, but I do remember the words she forsooth-verily spoke unto Li'l Snotty being drowned out by the screeching of *his* momma as she waddled into the battle. The tiny golden cross lassoed around her bulbous neck gleamed in the hot sun. Likewise, Mom's slightly more ornate cross returned a silent-but-righteous and fiery battle cry. It was on. Like Godzilla stomping to a Hibachi Barbeque picnic, the angry and feral woman took a sumo-stance in front of Mom, looming over my much smaller parent. Mom set her feet firm and glared up at the mega-Snooky, then smiled. Silently but lovingly, she placed her hand over the cross around her own neck. I feared for Godzilla.

Snooky — "Satan's Baby-Momma" — snatched her little angel away from Mom and buried the boy's head under her ample "boob-age" attempting homicide in her maternal comforting. "Leave my boy alone, you snooty Be-*#@ch!!!" Yeah. Snooky called Mom a "beach". I've paraphrased the terminology used, because, being raised by *my* mother, I dastn't use such coarse language.

"I was only trying to get Li'l Snotty to stop hitting his li'l sister. . . ."

"Yeah, right. Whatever, *be-*#@ch*. Why don't you leave *my* boy alone and go back to your 'Whoop-Tee-Du' gardening. All you rich-be-*#@ches are alike — your nose's always in other people's business." Snooky had the swirly shoulder/head action down pat years before it debuted on Jerry Springer.

"Ex-*cuuuse* me?" Mom quietly replied — and simply listening to her tone, I wanted to go for a bag of popcorn. This . . . was gonna be epic.

. . . but then the battle fizzled out before it even got going good. I watched the skan . . . "troubled single mother down on her luck who turns to a questionable life-style in a

last ditch effort to feed her cubs — Yada-Yada-Yada"
retreat back up the street to her fur-padded den. I'm sure
Snooky thought she'd won the war. But *I* knew *my* chihuahua
Mom wouldn't so easily let a leg go un-gnawed. It was a
let down watching a triumphant but well-fed Godzilla
flip-off Mom from the safety of her low-rent lair. Still . . . I
felt a bad moon rising. But since Creedence Clearwater
Revival had yet to be "born", I had no idea the horrible
depth my fears could sink, nor the unreal terrors of the
coming dawn. Eeeep?

The next day, Dad was at the curb, ready to pick me up
from school. He a strange smile on his face. The drive was
short and happy — I adored my dad and the one hour of the
day I had him all to myself, but. . . . We arrived home to an
empty house.

"Where's Mom?" I asked.

"Busy."

"Busy doing what?"

"Don't worry about it. It's you and me for the night, kid."

"Okay. . . ." This was a true and absolutely foreign
experience. I'd have hummed "Doo-doo-DOO-doo" — but
again . . . Twilight Zone had likewise not yet crawled from
the innards of Rod Sterling's skull.

"What's for dinner?"

"Pizza." Meaningless Factoid: The first pizza I ever ate.
Ever. Ever-Ever.

"Well . . . okay, then. . . . What's Mom eating?"

"Beans."

~*~

Apparently — so went the story — while I was at school,
Mom and Snooky returned to the middle of the street to
continue the "Gunfight At The OK Corral". Mom was loaded

for bear . . . or more precisely, loaded for Snooky. The "discussion" got animated. Someone probably pulled a weapon — no doubt, Mom. Finally, the police were called. Probably took an hour or two for the law to arrive, what with the great two block distance they had to cover. Even in "Mayberry Days", the police avoided patrolling Second Street. They knew what lived there — and this was *years* before anyone knew about neighborhood "hotspots". True "crime" — as we know it — had yet to be invented.

The police begrudgingly responded. A quarter got tossed into the air — Snooky caught it — and they arrested Mom. "Beans" was Dad's way of telling me my Sunday School teacher mother was spending the night in jail.

As it turned out, Dad had fought very hard to keep Mom from jail. Even Sheriff Ed *and* his "Jail-Matron" wife — both personal friends of Dad — were tirelessly trying to reason with Mom: "If you just admit remorse, the Judge says you'll go free — *Today!!!*"

"Ain't gonna do it."

Dad pinched the bridge of his nose. He'd heard this Top 40 hit before. Many times. "Give it up, Ed. She'll never listen to reason. It just ain't in 'er."

The Sheriff threw up his hands while his wife shook her head. Sheriff Ed showed Mom her purse, which they held in lock-up, and said: "Would you like to have this in your cell?"

Mom smiled sweetly at her friend. "Yeah . . . Thank you. That'd be nice."

"Well . . . you can't. Unless you allow Lawrence to take this home . . ." He removed an item from the purse. "For safe-keeping."

Mom saw what Sheriff Ed held in his hand. "Ain't gonna do it."

It was a tear gas gun — It was a freakin' tear gas gun. When she was arrested, they'd allowed her to bring the unsearched purse into the jail. Again — "Mayberry Days".

Sheriff Ed turned to Dad. "Lawrence? Please sneak this out in your pocket — All hell'll break loose if the judge knows she's got it."

"Nope — *Ain't gonna let 'im! My* purse stays with *me* — and *everything* in it *stays* in it as well!"

When Mom stated her opinion, she might as well have been carving on the cave wall. Mom held strong opinions throughout her life — *literally* from birth on. Legend has it, at two years of age, she ran buck-naked down the well-traveled Kentucky road in front of the family's tiny grocery store. Simply because she *could*. Grandpa was utterly mortified when all of his friends — gathered for a card game on the store's front porch — laughed themselves silly. "Bet *you* can't do that, Frank!"

Listening to Mom's set-in-stone determination to keep her purse, Sheriff Ed shrugged his shoulders. "Women . . . . What ya gonna do?" He shook his head at Dad. "Well . . . if she keeps her mouth shut about it, maybe Judge Ernest won't know . . . ."

Minutes later, led into court, Mom took her seat and glanced up at Judge Ernest. She set her jaw. I'm quite sure *Dad* knew this couldn't end well.

The Judge read the charges aloud . . . . Basically — the charges concerned Mom's attack on a perfectly innocent & virginal Snooky . . . *and* resisting arrest.

Judge: "Having read the charges . . . I'm inclined to dismiss this case to time served — this afternoon. *If* you'll simply say you're sorry. And promise not to do it again."

"Ain't gonna do it."

Judge: "Now, Mrs. Stepp. . . . Wouldn't you like to return home to your family tonight? All you have to do is apologize — I'll drop the charges — and you can leave with your husband."

Mom firmly set her jaw. "Ain't gonna do it."

Judge Ernest mirrored Mom's defiant stance and set *his* jaw. "And *why* are you being so stubborn?"

"Ain't gonna do it. They won't let me have my purse and I'll say no more on the matter."

Judge Ernest: (dropping gavel) "Contempt of court. Remanded to the matron until you can apologize to the poor young mother you viciously attacked. Enjoy your stay with us, Mrs. Stepp."

~*~

Next morning, while I was at my school-desk, Mom was again brought before Judge Ernest. Even though I wasn't there, I imagine Mom looked bright as a daisy — bright-eyed and as bushy-tailed as a Sunday School Teacher's expected to be when they face down the Great Satan. She feared no man. However, in the back row of wooden seats, Dad sat in the small courtroom. Fearing for the judge.

Judge: (smirking) "Mrs. Stepp. . . . I hope you had a pleasant night. Did you sleep well? Did your accommodations meet with your approval?"

"Tolerable. Slept like an *innocent* baby. Don't like beans, much, though. And they won't let me have my purse."

Judge: (smiling benevolently) "Wouldn't you like to return home to your family tonight? All you have to do is apologize — I'll drop the charges — and you can leave with your husband. What say? Let's settle this with a contrite and Christian heart, as the good Lord would want us to do."

"Ain't gonna do it."

Now, it was Judge Ernest's turn to pinch the bridge of his nose. "Mrs. Stepp. . . . *Why* won't you just apologize and be over and done with this un-Christian-like mess?" He shook his wizened head at her womanly folly and sent a knowing wink out into his courtroom.

Mom smiled. She smiled her best Sunday-go-to-meetin' smile. "So, Your Honor . . . You and the good Lord want me to apologize. And you wonder why I'm not gonna do it. Wanna know why I won't apologize? *Really* wanna know? *Cause Jesus knows. . . .*"

"Jesus . . . knows?" The judge was practically speechless — perhaps for the first time in his ethically questionable career. "*Jesus knows?*"

Mom merely smiled and nodded. Standing beside her, Sheriff Ed's wife, the matron, lowered her head and snickered, so softly only Mom heard.

When Mom spoke again, her words rang out into the small courtroom. As loudly as she could — given she only had half her vocal cords remaining, due to surviving cancer some eight years before — Mom enunciated every word for the benefit of the elected county official who sat in righteous judgment of her un-Christian act.

"Cause it was *you* Jesus and I see going up the alley to Snooky's every Wednesday and Friday night."

If that ever-proverbial pin had dropped, everyone in the courtroom and probably out in the courthouse hallway could have heard it. I'm quite sure Dad sat with his mouth agape — catching flies.

Judge Ernest: (dropping gavel) "I hold you in Contempt of Court. Fine waived. Mrs. Stepp? Get the hell outta my courtroom."

XX SIW Goes Platinum

The night of Mom's delivery from the Floyd County "Lion's Den", dinner was at Burger Chef on State Street. Much lamented, but long gone. It was *good* with *real* food — plastic food simply didn't exist in "Mayberry Days". I'm sure Mom enjoyed her meal immensely as we munched our burgers in absolute and total safety — she finally had her purse back.

XX and OO

Janet Wolanin Alexander

Early August had been unusually wet, so one day, during a break in the weather, I decided to sneak in a trail ride on my horse, Highlander. Despite my dwindling energy and the overcast sky, I put off some work and quickly drove to the stable to tack him up.

We headed into the forest around 6:30 pm. The comfortable temperature, dearth of biting insects, and threat of rain revitalized our youthful daring. I had retained enough maturity, however, to securely tie my poncho behind my saddle in the event of a sudden downpour.

After meandering through the woods from the valley up to a favorite ridge trail we'd not trod in a while, we turned left. The trail had slimmed down from its old fire road girth; soft earth topping most of the gravel that had been laid down a few years ago and was now ground in. The sandstone dirt was moist, but not muddy, and it matched Highlander's chestnut mane and coat. The gauntlet of overhanging branches sprinkled us continuously with water collected from the morning's storm. We were alone, just him and me, perfect company in our private world.

The vegetative green accenting Highlander's red began to dim. Birdsong transitioned to insect song — the towhee's "drink your tea" to cricket chirp. By the time we got to the end of the trail and turned around, it was twilight. We gaily ran back the ridge and started our darkening descent to the lake in the valley. I have good night vision, but, as hard as I tried, I couldn't see anything clearly. I squinted, slid my glasses down my nose, rubbed my nearsighted eyes, and still nothing focused. I was about to fling off my glasses in frustration when I realized that we were traveling through the condensation of a humungous cloud!

Like a ghost, it was invisible, yet somehow obscured everything it contained and was felt more than seen. But, not physically, as I cover up when I ride to avoid getting scratched, sunburned, bitten, and stung — only the skin on my lower face, neck, and wrists is exposed.

I felt my entry into and exit out of the cloud emotionally. It's hard to put into words. Imagine the surprise of a helium balloon or a kite being slowly and gloriously released from its long, but still-held, tether to dance in the air. Then, like a yoyo spun to the far end of its orbit, being unexpectedly and slowly pulled back to reality. Or, picture yourself, at the base of a dive, being released by the water's pressure and allowed to slowly float back to the surface. It's a brief, rare, out-of-your-element voyage followed by reentry into the familiarity of normalcy.

It was still twilight when Highlander and I emerged from the cloud. The twilight soon merged undetectably into dusk. And the dusk imperceptibly transitioned into darkness. Three happy hours after departure, we could see the barn's pole light in the distance, then, as we drew closer, the flashlight beam of the barn manager coming out to see if we were okay.

Okay?! Highlander was ready to get naked, roll in the pasture, and eat supper. And I was in seventh heaven! A spell had been cast — I felt more tranquil and more deeply relaxed than I had in a very long time.

I love riding my steed in the woods, especially at dusk.

Highlander, I should rename you Magic!

Madcap Midwestern Mythologies

Brett Alan Sanders

Napoleon Bonyparte's Ohio River Odyssey

George Washington's old war buddy the *Marqwis of Laffeeyette* went sailing down our local waterway one bright, resplendent morning after the dark clouds of the Revolution had all done cleared up. But by nightfall, round-about the time of that little disturbance of 1812, he found himself shipwrecked along those jagged shores. At a place now called Laffeeyette Spring — unjustly, considering who it was saved his sorry French butt! Laffeeyette, anyways, along with ship and crew, was near sucked down the throat of that mighty, raging whirlpool that in its day was called *Polly Feemus*'s *Eye*. Or by some folk, the Eye of the Cyclops.

To the unfortunate and helpless Frenchman's rescue (amidst all the thundering and flashing of lightning; despite the beating and pelting of raindrops the size of Fourth-of-July rockets, star-spangled and bursting in air), my great-great-grandpappy Napoleon Bonyparte come a-running.

Or *Napoleon Bonyparte Sanders*, I should maybe clarify, lest you accuse me of making up imperial genealogies. He was about half or a quarter Inkan, I've heard tell. Or Kaldean, or Kickapooan, something like that. Come up from across the river in Old Kaintuck. Most likely, Momma says (she was a Sanders girl before marrying a Polk), it was by his own momma or his grandmom that he got that particular red-flowing Indian blood.

This one's never been no one's emperor, in other words. Just to be clear. But he's strong and wiry like a *calavera*-skeleton on Mexican Day of the Dead. Folks just call him Bones. On account of the middle name, it's true, but more for always being so doggone skin-n-bony.

When Bonyparte come to the European traveler's rescue, anyways, it was might-near a hopeless cause. But that bonyfide American deliverer, trailblazing pioneer and confidant of Dan'l Boone himself (lumberjack companion, too, in more innocent times, to Paul Bunyan and his Blue Ox, Babe), that old rapscallion Bones seen it more as a "bootstrap moment," is what he said. And since Laffeeyette's Frenchified straps wasn't big enough for this particular vast and rugged Wilderness, my old grandpappy felt it behooven on him to pull up the poor fella with his own sturdier ones. Them that's got more in good sense and practical know-how's got a whale of a responsibility in this madcap world of ours.

The marqwis's sorry old noggin and a single raised arm was all there was of him still visible above the vortex's mud-streaked white spray when our almost naked (save for breechcloth and coonskin cap) and gray-horsed paladin come riding onto the scene. And our brave American Bonyparte leapt right in. Perceiving, right off the bat, that bringing that *escargoat*-eatin snail-smacker out alive would take an Olympic-style dive into the unholy and not-so-fragrant maelstrom. Leaving his handsome steed behind on dry ground and throwing himself in, even knowing that it'd take more'n a Hero's luck and iron gut to torpedo the whole distance down into those malodorous depths. Deep down into the foul, bile-inducing ooze of Dame Polly's half-blind

Cyclops Eye. Without even a nose plug to keep from spilling his lunch and further clouding up the already polluted and poisoned watery habitat.

Decked out in that rock-solid flesh of his, Bonyparte just dove in. And first, having scarcely pierced the noxious foaming surface, he set to orienting himself within an intricate maze of woven mud and river grasses. A colossal underwater Labyrinth like the one George Rapp and his German-born religious communalists had done built themself out of gigantic shrubs on the up-and-above ground over yonder at Harmony-on-the-Wabash, where my fourth-grade Indiana History class once took a field trip.

Our champion Bonyparte, anyways, our exemplary Napoleon of the Ohio River Valley, with nary a weapon but the strength of his rough-n-ready arms, went down like a vulture fit as a fiddle for the virulent feast on a bloody, maggot-ridden corpse. No sooner'n he's found himself in that not-so-sweet extremity, he commenced right in to wrassling the muscular, female *Minitower* with its Cyclops Eye, the One-Eyed Minitower that was chained up there guarding the secret dark heart of that watery inferno. Covered in muck and slimy riverweed, circling face to face, mano a mano, in hand-to-hand combat with that snaky-haired Medusa with the pus-filled Orb and giant toothpick-sharp devil horns, our very own frontier Napoleon takes her tangled locks in one hand and a single horn in the other and sets the raging She-Bull, or Minitower-Cyclops, or Amazon Woman in perpetual motion. Spinning her round and around she goes, gaining momentum till the quantum pull of distant planets sends her spiraling, chains and all, plumb out of the water and into deepest space. Converging on this fast-contracting black hole — Double-X marks the spot! — where the great cosmic dance of particles (and suchlike) of dark and light materials ignite in an infinitesimal-brief flash of illuminating, sparkling, bedazzling luminescence. Then this great sucking sound in the sky and the immense, irreversible vanishing act of all that matter immediately surrounding (and including) Polly F's rancid Eyeball.

My great-great-grandpappy of the bony parts, deliverer and protector of weak, pantywaist, or otherwise Frenchified humanity, before he'd hardly let go of the Minitower's appendages, went to grabbing and taking good hold on old Laffeeyette and all his ship and crew. Tucking them in towards his bony bosom so's they wouldn't, also, wind up in that genie's bottle of a black hole with their hideous abductor. Setting them all down on dry land, then, soon as the coast was clear.

And that's how this jocund little watercourse of ours got itself washed clean of that whole class of mythical, pus-oozing monstrosities and vermin as used to be all the time a-haunting it.

Still Life With Peanut Butter
Marian Allen

They say it's an ill wind that blows no good, and Max Carton's murder proved it.

Mamie didn't even think about the death until her young boarder, business partner and future sister-in-law, Florence Adagio, called it to her attention.

"Listen!" Florence bounced around to kneel on the couch, Kindle clutched in both hands, shouting over the sofa's low back and across two rooms. "This is just up your — Oh, crap!" She pivoted and slouched into silence.

Mamie, although she had heard every word and nuance, strolled out of the kitchen and said, "Did you say something, dear?"

"No." Florence's tone was sullen, but held an edge of possible hope. "Something exciting, but never mind. We can't do it. It's right around the *wedding*."

The loathing that infused the word *wedding* twisted Mamie's heart. If Florence turned against the wedding, Bennie might have second thoughts, and Bennie was probably Mamie's last hope of not dying a spinster.

"If you say so, dear," Mamie said, knowing that pressing for details would only make Florence more tightlipped.

"Well. . . ." Florence turned around again, holding her Kindle so Mamie could read it, if she came closer. "Here."

"You tell me about it, sweetheart. I leave the electronics to you."

Florence flipped the device around and said, "Okay, you remember when that man was found dead in a tub of shelled peanuts at Jumbo All-Natural? That little rinky-dink peanut butter factory that all the schools take field trips to?"

"Vaguely. Didn't they shut down?"

"Just long enough to disinfect everything. Then they opened again, but nobody wanted to buy their stuff because of the dead body."

"Did the peanuts kill him?" Mamie itched to take the Kindle and look up the article for herself, but she had carefully cultivated her tech-helpless image. She wasn't about to let anybody think she was capable of handling anything she could fob off onto them.

"Peanuts aren't generally homicidal." In a squeaky voice, Florence said, "I'm a peanut with a gun! Your money or your life!"

Mamie made herself laugh along. "He might have been allergic, you know. Or he might have been smothered under them."

Florence gave her an admiring look. "He might have." She skimmed the article. "No, he was 'bludgeoned'. That means walloped upside the head."

"I know what 'bludgeoned' means, dear."

"But that's not the important part. The important part is this: Jumbo is having a recipe contest. The winner gets a year's supply of peanut butter in your choice of creamy or crunchy, *pluh-uh-us* ... your picture and recipe on the labels of Jumbo All-Natural for a year and a featured spot on Nightly News at Nine preparing the recipe."

Now Mamie understood Florence's excitement. The two

of them did a weekly webcam cooking show, and Florence was always looking for a way to "take it to the next level".

Jumbo was only a local company, but the connection to a murder would surely gather some national attention. Even if it didn't, a featured spot on the local news would be something they could put in their video portfolio.

"And the contest would interfere with the wedding?"

"It starts today and runs to the week before. And the television thing is The Day. So there's a golden opportunity shot in the butt."

It certainly looked that way. Mamie swallowed bitter disappointment but said, "Such is life," and went back to watching her potatoes roast and her chicken fry.

Peanut butter. Now that she had it in her head, she couldn't stop thinking about it. *Peanut butter bon-bons would be nice for dessert.* She had several recipes for them. . . .

The doorbell rang. Mamie glanced at the clock. Five sharp. *Time for Bennie.* She waited until Florence opened the door, then hustled into the living room patting her hair as if worried about making an attractive appearance.

She caught Florence in the act of withdrawing a hand from Bennie's arm, exchanging a meaningful glance with him. Of course, Florence was going to try to get Bennie to postpone the wedding until after the contest. Mamie felt her face redden, but made herself smile as if blushing with pleasure.

Bennie raised her hand and kissed it, then embraced her and kissed her cheek.

"Y-you sssmell g-good enough to eat," he said, still stammering from the tension of his job.

Mamie led him to "his" chair. "Sit down and put your

feet up and relax, Dearest. Let Florence make you a drink while I finish supper."

Florence followed her into the kitchen to fill the ice bucket, avoiding her eye and humming nonchalantly, then went back to mix Bennie's bourbon and cola.

"Wwwwwwhat's up?" Bennie asked over the tinkling of the ice, but Florence shushed him. After that, the only sounds coming from the living room were the occasional hiss from a whispered conversation.

Think, Mamie, think!

~*~

When she called Florence and Bennie to set the table and get the dinner drinks, they all chatted aimlessly about their days, but a faint buzz of tension exhilarated the atmosphere. Mamie concentrated on keeping her expression bland — difficult to do when one expected what was going to be proposed and had planned how to undercut it.

It wasn't until dinner was underway that Bennie spoke, ascending into formality, his way of combating his stutter, "M-my dear, there may be some difficulty with our wedding plans. With the date, you know."

"Oh, I do hope not! Because I've been thinking about this wonderful contest Florence told me about. Did she tell you?"

"Why. . . ."

Florence, always quicker than Bennie, said, "What were you thinking, Sister Mamie?"

She told them, and enjoyed watching Bennie's eyebrows rise and Florence's jaw drop. She had stolen this march, for certain.

A reception sit-down dinner for thirty, catered by the bride, with every course featuring peanut butter.

A major affair, bigger than she'd been able to back Bennie into before, and right on schedule.

Jumbo's PR Director, Susan Breeden, met Mamie and Florence in the lobby and led them through to the factory floor. In spite of its name, Jumbo was a small operation — just a couple of steps up from a mom-and-pop. They ran only two shifts. The production line was closing down as they walked it. Machines switched off, employees shut away supplies and scrubbed their areas so the cleaning crew could do the general stuff. So Susan said in passing.

"Sacks of cleaned, shelled peanuts come in here, then they're moved over to there, where they're roasted. We roast our own peanuts, to assure quality and consistency and that special Jumbo touch."

Mamie smiled and let the blather run past her ears. She wanted to see the bin the dead body had turned up in.

". . . only pure cane sugar, never beet sugar or corn syrup," Susan assured them, "and the finest sea salt. No artificial additives or preservatives except for the least possible touch of stabilizer to prevent separation."

Florence said, "That's why Jumbo is perfect for our show. The best ingredients are the purest and simplest. Right, Mamie?"

"Absolutely right."

The machine that squirted the peanut butter into jars made Mamie a little nauseous. She couldn't help thinking of the picture she'd seen on the internet of a peanut in the shell sitting on a tiny little toilet seat with a straw leading from the pot into a jar of peanut butter. It had been funny at the time.

All the workers in paper shower caps and goggles and plastic gloves and face masks didn't help. They were probably supposed to be all hygienic and everything, but they looked like they were working with toxic waste.

"Very clean," Florence said.

"We've never had less than the Board of Health's top rating," Susan said.

In spite of herself, Mamie had to give her A Look.

Susan saw it and bristled.

"The thing that happened didn't happen *in* the factory. It was out in the staging area of the loading dock. And it had nothing to do with our product, it was a by-product on the way to a farmer."

"Eww," escaped from Mamie's mouth, an expression she had picked up from her young lodger. Florence bit down on a smile and shook her head behind Susan's back.

"Look." Susan stopped walking and her lips clamped shut, as if one part didn't work without the other. She tapped her foot, which seemed to rev her jaw up again, and said, "Mr. Mateo doesn't want us to dwell on the . . . incident, but I think it's important that you two, of all people, see the whole picture."

The PR Director took Mamie's and Florence's elbows and steered them around machines and workers and out an open door that was more like a missing wall.

There were three areas. One was stacked with brown cardboard boxes with JUMBO ALL-NATURAL printed on the side. Another held red plastic 55-gallon drums and the last had blue drums of the same size.

Susan pointed from one bunch of containers to another to another. "Peanut butter, skins and fragments, hearts." Before anyone could say *Eww* again, Susan clarified, "The shelled peanuts we get still have those red skins on them? So we have a machine that shucks them off. We passed it just as we came onto the floor. We sell them and any peanut scraps and shell fragments that come off with them to Avery Organic Farms to feed their hogs. They're local. The hearts of the peanuts can be bitter, so we have a machine that separates those before the peanuts are crushed and sell those to Michael's Songbird Suet. Also local." She shoved a finger toward the red barrels. "That's where the man was found. In one of the by-product barrels. In with the skins. Nothing to do with our product at all, but the media had a field day with us."

"It was a shame," Florence said. "Everybody knows Jumbo's reputation for quality and purity."

They were just turning back to the work area when a man jogged up the loading dock steps and clocked in. The minute he came into view, the word *crooked* flashed across Mamie's mind. Something in the way he carried himself, a twist at the corner of his mouth, a sideways glance gave him away. He smiled and waved as nearby workers greeted him, ducked his head and touched his Patriots ball cap to Susan and Florence and Mamie in a perfunctory bow. His gaze and Mamie's met and his sharpened and shifted. Somebody, seeing the direction of his attention, said something to him. He nodded and smiled.

Mamie smiled back, hoping her instant dislike didn't show as plainly as his instant defensiveness did.

Susan said, "That's Pete, the night watchman. He used to come in after the cleaning crew left until . . . the incident. Now we have him come in before the second shift clocks out. It never occurred to anybody that we needed to watch the plant 24/7. It's been a PR nightmare."

The Director smiled hopefully at the partners. "Your wonderful wedding feast is just what we need to start good buzz again. The Kitchen Bitches will move Jumbo into the twenty-first century." She said the show's name self-consciously, as if she weren't used to using such language at work, but a naughty twinkle in her eye said the word *bitch* was no stranger to her lips.

Susan led them through the rest of the tour. They shook hands with the line foreman, accepted Honorary Peanut Butter Inspector badges and had their pictures taken for publicity.

Mamie wished she never had to look another peanut in the eye again.

~*~

The next day, a grumpy Florence navigated while Mamie drove. "Isn't pork cheating?"

"I don't cheat, Sweetheart," Mamie replied with a deceptive mildness that didn't fool Florence and wasn't meant to.

"Naturally, I don't mean *you*. I mean Jumbo. Isn't everything supposed to be based on peanut butter?"

"It doesn't have to be pure nothing *but* peanut butter, just made *with* peanut butter. Or peanuts. Besides, they figured since the hogs at Avery Farms are fed partly on by-products from Jumbo, I should use some Avery meat."

"But why do we have to drive out and pick it up? If they want you to use it, they ought to deliver it."

Mamie huffed sympathetically and crooned, in the tone of an adult consoling a disappointed child, "I know, sweetheart. And why did it have to be today, of all days? You should have let me come alone. I probably wouldn't have gotten lost. Or Bennie could have come."

Florence would have hated either of those alternatives worse than she hated missing an Evil Dolly Boys concert. Grudgingly, she said, "I'm the publicity side of the partnership.

It has to be me." With that, her morose air lightened, obviously lifted by the thought of her own indispensability.

Mamie parked between the farmhouse and the locker plant just as Jackson Avery *putt-putt*ed up on a tractor. He was a big man, built like a Budweiser horse in overalls and a ratty straw hat, face creased with age and sun, fingers gnarled by work.

"Hi, there! You must be the bride." He stuck a hand out to Florence, then grinned at Mamie and said, "And you must be the proud mamma."

Both women laughed. Mamie took his hand and said, in a tone meant to convey her gracious forgiveness for his blunder, "Everybody makes that mistake. *I'm* the bride. Florence is my baby sister-in-law-to-be."

"Oh! Oh, sorry," Avery said. "Ripe peaches are the best, am I right?"

They all laughed again.

Avery kept up a line of cheerful patter as he showed them around the farm. He deferred to Mamie, which would have been flattering if she hadn't felt patronized, as well. Florence was being patronized but *not* deferred to, but that was because Florence was young, which made the respect he showed Mamie due to Mamie's being . . . not young.

The hogs were raised on Avery's farm, then shipped to a processing plant. The wrapped, labeled and frozen packages of meat were shipped to the locker plant for sale and not-frozen hams were shipped back for smoking. Ham was what Mamie wanted: applewood-smoked sliced paper-thin.

They ended the tour back outside by one of the pigpens.

"Hogs don't smell, if you keep them clean," Jackson said, reaching over a fence to scratch a doomed porker behind the ears. "Come over here and pet her and then smell your hand."

"No, thank you," Mamie said. "I have a rule never to make friends with anything I intend to kill and eat."

In fact, this little visit was causing her to reconsider including ham on the menu at all. Clean hogs did smell — they smelled like pork.

Avery made a sound of polite dismissal, stroking the hog's back while it grunted and snuffled. "It don't matter to her. She lives good and she's happy and when she goes, she won't know what hit her. A person could do worse."

Mamie shivered in the sun.

"Besides, what you'd get hasn't been on the hoof for some time. It's been butchered and smoked and aged. Better when it's aged."

If that was supposed to be a compliment, Mamie could do without it.

"So that's the operation," Avery said. "Let's go back to the office and talk some turkey. I mean *ham*."

Florence and Mamie giggled as if they didn't realize he said the same thing every time he negotiated price with a customer.

They followed him along the dirt path to the barn-shaped building that held the smokehouse, industrial freezer, Country Store and office. As she followed Florence inside, Mamie caught a glimpse of a green car pulling up and a flash of blue and red hopping out. She paused, inspecting and smelling the white clematis climbing the lattice by the office door, and watched the red and blue figure.

It was the man they'd seen at Jumbo the night before — Pete, the night watchman.

What's he doing here? Moonlighting? Or is it

sunlighting, if you take a second job besides night work?

He glanced her way, then closed his car door soundlessly and glided through an entrance farther along the building. If she remembered correctly from Avery's tour, it was the holding room for the deliveries from Jumbo.

Hmmmm. Sneakiness is always intriguing.

"Coming, Mamie, dear?"

"Oh, it's just too pretty to go indoors. Besides, you're the one with the head for business. I'd just be in the way. I'll meet you at the car."

Florence would like that. She really *did* have a head for business, and the fact that people — especially men past a certain age — tended to underestimate such a dewey-eyed young thing didn't hurt her bargaining power.

Mamie vacillated between creeping behind Pete and breezing after him, acting innocent and unaware. She decided innocent but quiet might be the best course. If she caught him at something — putting growth hormones in the hog slop or whatever — and he didn't see her, she could ease away and keep it to herself unless she needed it for leverage some time and some way. If he did see her, she could pretend she was just having a clueless look around and had no idea what she'd witnessed.

The inside of the building was nearly as bright as the outdoors. A thin layer of coarse sawdust covered the floor, the fresh smell of pine and sassafras covering the less appealing odors from the pen out back.

Pete wasn't in sight.

Stacks of red barrels to either side of the door made a short corridor. A door in the far wall swung open to the outside, moving slightly in the gentle breeze. Clueless face firmly fixed, in case Pete came back in, Mamie walked into the room.

~*~

She woke up drooling into her collar in the pitch dark. The air was thick and stale. She snuffled up a deep breath and coughed as flecks and scraps invaded her mouth. Dizzy and disoriented, she flailed her arms — tried to, but struck hard surfaces. She cried out and pressed her hands against what they had hit, something curved at her side, something flat above her head.

And she knew where she was. She was in one of the barrels of by-products shipped to the farm from Jumbo, just like the man who had been found dead at the factory. *Dead!* A sense of injustice flooded her. If she had suspected Pete was involved with murder, she never would have followed him. Why couldn't he have settled for just being moderately crooked? Something shameful but not actually dangerous?

She pushed against the lid and almost passed out again from the pain in the back of her head. The lid didn't even give. In fact, she just pushed herself further down into the peanut drek.

What was Pete's plan? Had he left her for dead, or had he left her to die? The air was already stuffy. Is this what he had planned for What's-His-Name, the dead guy, except somebody found the body before he could ship it to the farm?

Body in barrel, barrel at farm — and now what?

Did pigs eat people? She thought she'd heard they would eat anything. Not *live* people, surely. But did they just empty the barrels into the pig-feeding places — the mangers or troughs or whatever they called them — or did they put all the feed elements into a big bin and mix them up? She thought she had seen something about a machine that cooked the feed all up into a slush. Kind of like peanut butter.

How long have I been in here? Just because it was dark in the barrel didn't mean it was dark outside. If she'd been gone very long, Florence would have been looking for her. Had Florence been clobbered, too?

Or had Florence realized something was wrong and gone for the police? Was Florence about to rescue her poor, helpless, captive older partner, hogging — no pun intended — all the glory?

No! She worked her way around the rim of the lid, rapping it with what force she could, given her cramped position, until she found a spot where it was just a little loose. She wiggled herself into a more stable placement and pushed, in spite of her throbbing head, until she raised a crack of light and fresh air. Piggy or not, the air smelled wonderful. It was still broad daylight. Maybe she hadn't been unconscious very long.

She didn't hear the footsteps until they were almost beside the barrel. A pry bar thrust through the crack she'd made and jiggered the lid up with squeaks and groans from the plastic.

If the pry bar belonged to rescue, she wanted to be awake, to tell them she had been effecting her own escape before they arrived. If it belonged to Pete, she might be better off pretending to be asleep, to catch him off-guard.

She closed her eyes.

Light flooded in as the lid was removed. A hand *shooshed* into the by-products and ran along her leg.

Her eyes flipped open to see Pete leaning over the rim of the barrel.

"I *beg* your pardon," she said frostily. *It's bad enough*

being bludgeoned, let alone being groped.

Pete pulled back so violently, the barrel went over with him. It rolled, peanut skins, shells and fragments strewing loopily along its path.

Mamie scrambled out and to her knees, sagging from dizziness and pain.

Pete, pry bar raised, charged at her. When he got close enough to swing, Mamie ducked aside and threw a double handful of peanut scraps into his face. He gasped, gagged and coughed, stumbling past her, pry bar landing somewhere with a clang.

"See how *you* like a face full of by-products," she said.

She used the barrel to lever herself to her feet. Tried to, rather, but it rolled from under her hand and she slid back to the floor. Just as the barrel went rolling, Pete turned around, wiping his streaming eyes.

"Don't make me hurt you," he rasped, voice rough with the scraps he'd inhaled. Then the barrel hit his ankles and he windmilled, trying to keep his balance.

Mamie managed to make it to her feet and gave him another double handful of scraps.

"Okay," she said. "I won't."

Pete gargled and coughed. Mamie stepped up to him and slapped him hard enough to spin him around.

She lifted a foot, planted it firmly against his backside and pushed, watching with satisfaction as he went headfirst into the wall, keeled over backwards and bounced off the barrel.

He groaned and stirred, then went still.

Jackson Avery's voice floated in from the parking lot. "Ladies? Miss Florence? Miss Mamie? Where'd you get to?"

Before she could decide whether she should hide from him, his big frame filled the doorway.

The cornpone grin fell from his face. "Oh, my lord, what happened here? You're hurt! What happened to Pete? Where's the little girl?"

It took her a minute to realize he meant Florence.

"Pete knocked me unconscious and put me in that barrel, but I got out and knocked him down. The last time I saw Florence, she was heading for your office."

"We finished our business and she came looking for you."

She imagined Florence stuffed in a barrel of hog slop, her eyes big black Xs like a cartoon corpse's. *If she's dead, Bennie will never forgive me.*

Jackson dug into one of his overall pockets and pulled out a cell phone.

"Don't touch that pry bar he was after you with," he said. "That'll have his fingerprints on it. Get another one off the wall and start opening these here barrels in case he put her in one, too. Soon as I get hold of the police, I'll help."

~*~

They opened seven barrels before they found Florence, out cold but with a much smaller lump than Mamie's. A police car took Bennie to meet the women at the hospital, where they were treated and where the police took their statements.

A Kitchen Bitches fan called the press, and Mamie, though she would have loved to tell all about her epic battle, had the consolation of uttering, at police insistence, that most official of non-statements, "No comment."

In time, they learned that Pete had used Jumbo as the drop point for his small-time drug operation and used his second job at Avery as the pick-up point. Max Carton, the corpse, had been a customer who stalked Pete until he figured out the drop. Pete caught him trying to take the whole delivery for himself and walloped him, meaning to knock him out but killing him instead. He stashed him in a barrel going to Avery's farm, hoping some idea of how to dispose of the body would come to him there. But somebody at Jumbo opened the barrel to see why it was so much heavier than the others, and found Carton's body.

The police also found the drugs in another barrel, but they put them back, hoping to follow Pete to his source. A thorough investigation of the Averys cleared them of any connection with the crimes. In fact, they had been informed of the sting and been sworn to secrecy, which Jackson insisted meant he had been deputized.

When Pete saw Mamie at the factory and then at the farm, he thought she was onto him. When she followed him on tiptoe, he was sure of it.

"He was right, of course," Mamie said to Bennie and Florence. "I knew the minute I saw him he was no good."

Florence said, "Oh, you did not know he was a drug-runner and a killer!"

"I didn't *know*, of course, dear, but I suspected. Then he bludgeoned the two of us and stuffed us into barrels. Repeating the same M.O., as they say on those frightening shows you watch. Of course, then he had to move the car, which meant he had to have the keys, which were in my purse, which he had tossed into the barrel with me, which meant he had to open my barrel and look for them, which gave me the chance I'd been waiting for."

"Tiger Princess!" Bennie put an arm around her and gently kissed her still-bandaged head. "Joan of Arc!"

"Whatever," said Florence. "Anyway, it's good for business."

Jumbo canceled the recipe contest and tried to drop sponsorship of the wedding banquet, but Florence held them to their contract. Nightly News at Nine had made Mamie, Florence, their webcam show and the upcoming wedding a regular Human Interest Feature. When other sponsors offered to buy out Jumbo's end of the contract, Jumbo changed their minds and called off their lawyers.

Bennie wondered aloud if it were in the best of taste to go ahead with the plan, given the seriousness of Pete's crimes.

"It's t-turning innto a m-media circus," he said.

"I know!" Florence rubbed her hands together in glee.

"Absolutely," said Mamie. "And what's a circus without peanuts?"

The Dinner Party
Michele Hubler

I knew this abandoned house, on the edge of a wood, would be the perfect spot. That rotting piece of clapboard, she'll be there. I dropped my scythe and worked the soft wood with my fingers. But she was a trickster. Out of the corner of my eye, I spied a tiny creature scurrying into a clump of johnsongrass.

I parted the blades gently. "There you are!"

A brown recluse returned my greeting warily. Her babies had hatched not too long ago from the looks of them. Mama recluse looked at me, her little eyes swiveling this way and that, concluded that I was neither prey nor predator, and went on about her business.

I fancy myself a self-taught spider expert, all my knowledge acquired through my keen powers of observation. Study only dulls the mind; my abilities to sense and detect had always been extraordinary and even now were as sharp as ever. My ex-wife would have hastened to disagree, and I will admit that sometimes one sees only what one wants to see. Perhaps I chose not to see her torrid and tawdry affair with my best friend and business partner.

While a life of selling insurance does prepare one for the horrors of existence, I found the real threats have two legs and two eyes, not eight. So, I spent my time crawling about attics, basements, and musty closets, treasuring each encounter with the clever and resilient creatures.

"There you are!" The female voice behind me was just shy of a bronchial breakdown, hollow with harsh edges. "You sure are a hard, uh, man to find."

Well now, there were a couple of things wrong right away. First, I was hardly what you could call a man. I was a ghost, a state change that I embraced some time ago. Second, most people couldn't see me. Something, I believe, about the arrangement of the rods and cones in their eyes. Oh, dogs and cats, spiders and other higher species could see me, but most humans couldn't unless I wanted them to. Then, there was the occasional exception who didn't *want* to see me.

"I'm speaking to you, sir."

I knew I didn't have anything to worry about, although that tone struck me as a trifle odd. This was an inconvenience, nothing more. There were spiders aplenty. I'd just get my scythe and take my leave of this gentlewoman. I reached for said farm implement, intending to offer my pleasantries and move along. My fingers closed on thin air.

"Looking for this?"

I turned toward my accidental companion, a woman of considerable girth with dark eyes shaded by heavy brows. Fine black hair covered her arms. (*It must be warm,* I thought. *Ah, summer in Georgia. It had been a great time to be alive.*) She lowered those formidable brows at me impatiently, a look I imagined the callow young man next to her had been treated to many times. The youth was holding my scythe behind his back and did not seem inclined to return it. He wore a white short-sleeved shirt with the collar open. There were sweat stains under his arms.

"Why, yes, thank you very much. That must be heavy. I'll just take it off your hands and be on my way, and we will be left with the fond memory of a pleasant encounter."

The boy looked at the lady next to him, whom I took to be his mother. She impatiently shook her head.

"You don't dress like Death. But, I guess, being Death, you can dress however you want."

At first, I thought she was insulting my garb. One can't help what one is wearing as a ghost. You are left with what you wore at the intersection of the old life and the new one, a fact which gives the mother's warning about wearing clean undergarments in good repair significant import. In my case, I had been clothed in black leather pants and jacket, with a black turtleneck to ward off the chill as I rode my motorcycle in the autumn countryside.

"Cat got your tongue?" asked the woman. "Death be not shy," she declaimed and then guffawed, swatting the boy's shoulder to signal her wit. He tittered nervously. "Don't be thinking of trying anything," she said to me. "We got your instrument of death right here. And I mean to keep it until you do right by me."

I was still confused. "What can I do for you, madam?"

"That's more like it. I know someone who should be dead. In fact, you should have taken her a couple of years ago, when she had pneumonia, and then when the chandelier fell on her." The smirk that accompanied this statement led me to believe that perhaps the chandelier being poorly anchored was not accidental.

"There was the hole with the snake inside, too, Momma. And the. . . ."

"That's enough, dear. No need to revisit past failures." To me: "Just do your job. That's all I ask."

It was dawning on me. She thought I was Death. Not for the first time, I cursed the fate that led me to that quaint country hardware store on that fall day.

~*~

On that brilliantly sunny October afternoon, I'd taken the motorcycle out to cruise the countryside on the hunt for arachnids. I began to feel a little nauseated, with a pain in my left jaw I attributed to recent dental work. I stopped at the store for a drink and, hopefully, some aspirin.

The storekeeper dug a couple of likely looking pills from his drawer and handed me a bottle of water. I tried to swallow but the tablets stuck in my throat.

"You okay, buddy?" asked a local gentleman, with a startling shortage of teeth and an excess of nose hair. "You don't look so good."

I was unable to provide him with the courtesy of a reply. I collapsed, grabbing the nearest thing to me, an item from a display of antique farm tools, namely the scythe. I awoke looking up at a crowd of faces clustered above me like the spokes of a web. I tried to speak, to reassure those kindly folk, but then, I spied an actual web in the northwest corner of the ceiling. Without thinking, scythe still in hand, I rose, determined to get a closer look at the arachnid architect of that structure. The crowd didn't part. They didn't need to. People say a window opens after you die, but as long as I keep a firm grip on the scythe, I'm too busy to notice the breeze.

~*~

"But, madam," I protested in as gentle a manner as I could muster, duty-bound as I was to inform her of her error. "You are mistaken. I am not Death. I am, in fact, one of his happy victims." I floated a languid hand toward the scythe. "That is the jess that keeps me firmly on my perch, if you will. It can do you no harm. But, it must be heavy. Let me take my burden and say adieu."

The young man jerked away the implement so quickly he nearly sliced his mother's forearm. "Watch it!" she barked.

I flinched until he slowly moved the tool back into range. The further I got from my tool, the weaker I felt. He'd seen it. He smiled.

"Oh, a smooth talker. I expected as much. Here's the thing. Melvin here saw you from the road. We're on the way to our intended, uh relative, right now. But, we took the time to stop and give you the chance to do right by us finally. When we saw you throw that thing there onto the grass and crawl around, why, we were interested. Very very interested. Downright fascinated. I said to Melvin, 'Get that thing. Death always has that with him. It must have some kind of power or something'." A slow smile spread like a virus over her face. "And, I believe it does. Melvin, honey, go stand over there." She indicated a spot about 20 feet on the other side of the house.

"No!" I gasped.

"It looks like I have your attention. After you send this person to her reward—"

"There's a reward, Momma?"

"Yes, Melvin, but not the kind you're thinking of. And don't interrupt again." She thumped him on the cheek. "As I was saying, you do what you should have done a couple of years ago, and you get your stick back. Deal?"

Ghosts, for all the popular literature, have little means of terminating a human life. We can hold only the lightest things, other than the thing we are holding when we transform, the scythe in my case. We can't assault a human. We could scare a person to death, but that didn't seem to be working for me in this situation. And without my scythe, I was truly vulnerable. It wasn't that I didn't think I would go to heaven if I let go of my earthly weight, but I didn't *want* to go to heaven. I just didn't think they'd have arachnids up there. All the paintings made it look like a wretchedly clean kind of place.

Wait. All was not lost. I had an idea.

"Of course, madam." I bowed. "Whatever you wish. I am eager to meet this ogress so deserving of a painful demise."

"Well, then stop yakking and come on."

"A moment, if you please." I bent and whispered an apology to the reclusive beauty, scooping her and her babies into my mouth.

"Momma! Death's eating spiders!"

"I don't care what you eat, but don't scare the boy." She leaned forward. The red stripes on her garment reminded me of bloody exclamation marks. "I'd figured you more of a steak kind of guy, but whatever. We're late." She looked at me. "I assume you can teleport yourself. We'll take the car. It's down the road about a quarter mile, first house on the left. Big yellow brick house. Can't miss it. Don't dawdle."

They turned and walked away. The boy stumbled over the uneven ground. His mom, rather than steady him, grabbed the scythe. I hurried after them, shrinking down to the size of a moth and attaching myself to the hood of her vehicle. I dared not adhere to my beloved farm implement. She was a woman of formidable instincts and I feared I was no match for her.

They turned into the driveway of a stately home, yellow brick to be sure. I flew off the automobile, resumed my original size behind a venerable oak, and stood waiting at the entrance gate. The boy, carrying my scythe, scampered from his side of the car, ran to his mother's door, and opened it. She accepted the rare courtesy as if she were the queen.

"Prompt. That's a good start." She muttered, not looking at me.

Inside the grounds, I expected a formal garden, complete with floribunda and boxwood shrubs. Instead, the area was given over to more humble flora, wildflowers and such. Something about the plants tugged at my consciousness, but I had too much on my mind to pursue a whimsical notion.

"See that?" The woman had seen my look of surprise at the garden. "That's just an example of the insanity, the cruelty this woman is capable of. Josiah, my husband, God rest his soul, and my Daddy treasured the roses, the irises, the azaleas. They're not even cold in the ground, when she tears it all out and plants weeds. Weeds! Criminal!"

"Hardly weeds, madam—" A couple of tiny spiders took advantage of the opening, so to speak, and scurried to freedom.

The boy gagged. His mother gently cuffed him on the ear.

"Hush!" Her eyes swiveled in my direction. "When I want your opinion, I'll ask for it. Keep your mind on your job. Watch my fork. When I drop it, that's the signal."

The door opened before our little party could ring the bell. A small pale woman dressed entirely in brown exclaimed in a voice as smooth and light as fine crystal, "Here you are! Margo and Melvin! I was afraid you weren't coming." She clapped her gloved hands. "Oh you shouldn't have. You know how I love antique farm tools." She reached for the scythe.

The boy pulled it away, cautiously this time, no doubt to avoid another thumping.

"Melvin, don't be rude! Well, dear sister-in-law Celia, you caught us. This *is* for you. But, I want to tell you about it before you go putting it on the wall. It's got quite a history." Margo frowned at her hostess' hands. "What's with the gloves, Jackie Kennedy?"

Celia's laugh was like the wind teasing the strings of a harp. "Oh, I feel so silly. I was working in the garden this morning and got a rash on my hands."

"Whatever. As long as it didn't get in the food," was Margo's surly reply.

"Not to worry." The tiny woman led the way down a dark dim hall paneled in walnut. The bun she wore at the base of her neck gleamed like smoky topaz. I felt my ire rising at the threat these two represented to this gentle creature.

"I can't wait to hear about the scythe. I love a good story. And dinner's all ready." She led us to a small, intimate room with a fireplace at one end. An elegant dining set dominated the room, with a serving table along one wall. A white cake, stunningly decorated, took pride of place on the table.

"What're we doing in here? Why aren't we in the dining room?"

"The dining room is so large and cold. This is much cozier, with just us." She smiled. "Please, sit." She swept a gloved hand toward the chairs and perched on her own at the head of the table, her back to the fireplace, which glowed merrily with a small fire. "I made the meal especially with you in mind. I hope you enjoy it."

The table was prettily set, with plain dishes, the better to show off the beauty of the feast. A glorious glazed chicken, stuffed with what looked like herbal dressing, was flanked by a salad, made, no doubt, with the very "weeds" Margo disparaged, crusty loaves of bread flecked with herbs, as well. Potatoes, and broccoli with carrots, all bursting with the goodness of the garden, completed the menu. Tall glasses of tea stood like faithful servants to quench the thirst of those enjoying the feast. It was a repast fit for royalty, more than these rascals deserved.

Incongruously, in front of the hostess who'd slaved over the magnificent meal, was a plate of crackers and a glass of plain water.

The two would-be murderers stood at the table. Melvin propped the scythe on the table, yanked out a chair, and plopped into it with a thud.

"Melvin."

"Oh, yeah." He jumped to his feet and pulled out a chair for his mother, then slammed his bottom back into his seat.

"Melvin, that's no place for the scythe."

I agreed with her. The blade still carried the evidence of its years of labor in the fields. To put that on the tabletop was an insult to the hostess.

"Hand it to me." Margo took it and carefully leaned it against the table on her left side.

I positioned myself behind them, the assassins, the better to see the signal. And, were I to be honest, to leap at any chance to rescue my poor farm implement and abscond with it.

"Mom, what's that?" The boy pointed a not-quite-clean finger at the salad.

"Don't be rude." She turned to her intended victim. "What is this? Looks like something I emptied out of the vacuum cleaner."

Celia smiled. "It was all harvested today. With my recent cancer diagnosis, and chemo treatment, I have vowed to live simply. From the abundance nature provides."

"Cancer? Chemo?" The words tumbled from Margo's mouth like gold from Midas' fingertips. She pretended to pick a bit of lint from her shoulder and threw a look of approval in my direction. "That's why you're eating that." She waved at the plate of crackers.

"I'm afraid so. A trifling of a stomach upset. But, enough about me. Eat. Enjoy. And, while you do, tell me about the scythe."

Margo launched into a skillfully woven lie about finding the scythe at an auction, and emerging victorious after a vicious round of bidding. As she spun the fiction, she stuffed her mouth with the dishes that her victim had prepared for her. Her fingers never left the worn handle of the scythe, my scythe.

Where was her fork? Every time the silver implement left my field of vision, I panicked. I was so anxious, I barely heard the dinner conversation. Ghosts don't have hearts to pound, instead we waver and shimmer and shrink when under stress. All the while watching for Margo's sign, trying to stay within range of my scythe, and keeping the restless spiders in check with my tongue, I also fretted about what this would mean if, at some future date, I did go through the legendary window. Is a murder committed after death still a sin?

Margo paused in her stream of lies, loaded fork in hand. "I knew you'd love it. I said to Melvin, 'Melvin,' I said, 'I have to have something special for our Celia. She has a singular place in our hearts'."

Celia sipped her water. "How sweet." One gloved finger artfully touched her heart.

The woman tapped the tines of her fork on the edge of

the plate for emphasis. "Why, just this afternoon, I was telling Melvin how much I was looking forward to this dinner. Wasn't I, son?"

"Yes, ma'am." He spoke around a mouth full of bread and chicken, the little hooligan.

Celia sighed and smiled, head tilted charmingly. "Yes. Me too. Even though I wasn't feeling quite up to par, there was no way I was going to cancel. Let's give your mother a chance to eat, Melvin. Tell me about school."

Melvin chewed and spit and whined about stupid teachers, mean kids, and dumb classes. The white linen tablecloth would never recover. Celia nodded and pursed her lips and rolled her eyes on cue.

The fork. Where was the fork? For the love of all arachnids, where . . . oh, there, Margo shoveled salad in her mouth. I could hear her chewing.

"Your cancer?" Margo blurted out over her son's lament about unfair grading practices. "Is it bad?" She practically rubbed her palms together in glee.

"Well," Celia lowered her eyes and toyed with the remaining crackers on her plate. "It's never good. But, I'm hopeful."

"Oh, me too," said Margo. "Right, Melvin?"

"I don't feel so good." The boy moaned a little.

"You must still be hungry." A consummate hostess, Celia nudged the dishes of chicken, salad, rolls, and vegetables toward her guests.

Melvin tried to lift his bread, but his fingers couldn't close on the item. "Mom," he mumbled as he dropped his head in his hands. "I'm dizzy. And I can't feel my legs."

Margo picked up her glass. Halfway to her mouth, the glass slipped from her hand. "I'm not. . . . We must be. . . ."

She leaned forward, as if to slide her chair back from the table. Her fork clattered to the floor. That was the actual utensil. Now, I was confronted with the virtual fork in the road. Now was time to gird my loins, to determine if I were to pass perpetuity in eternal damnation.

My path was clear. I was not going to allow that horrid woman to harm sweet, fragile Celia. I leaned forward and spit my tiny weapons of mass destruction onto Margo's neck. And then shoved some down the hellion's shirt, as well.

The dogs of war, or spiders in this case, had been loosed. I resolved I would leave this earth with some shred of integrity intact and defend those who knew not the threat that lurked.

I was ready for chaos, shrieks of pain, dire consequences meted out by the malevolent Margo.

I did not expect what happened next.

Which was nothing, really.

Margo wriggled some, slapping languorously at her shoulders and neck as the creatures, startled and fearful, bit the tender flesh. Melvin slumped forward, perhaps already a victim of my perfidy. One arachnid had made its way from its intended prey down to the tabletop, scurrying toward Celia. That lady bent over the tiny thing, examined it closely, laughed, and smashed it with her thumb. My affection for Celia diminished slightly.

By now, both mother and son had assumed the same posture, head down, face in plate. Melvin had broken his water glass. I worried a shard would pierce his eye. A crime committed in the commission of protecting the innocent was one thing. But I certainly didn't want to maim anyone.

I reached for the scythe, but Celia rose from her seat and grasped the tool. As she held the sharp blade aloft with one hand, she lifted the heavy heads of her sister-in-law, then her nephew, and leaned them back in their chairs. The boy did have a cut on his forehead. Celia ran a finger through the butter and swiped it over the cut. "There. That's better."

Celia gathered the dishes, contents and all, and threw them into the fire. The flames sizzled and sputtered, as if they were as taken aback as I was. Then, she carefully, finger by finger, peeled the gloves from her hands and tossed them into the fire, as well.

The table now cleared, she sliced a large piece of cake and ate while she watched her relatives pass into unconsciousness.

As I witnessed these macabre events unfold, I saw afresh in my mind's eye the plants in this woman's garden: monkshood, columbine, goat's rue, hollow Joe-Pye weed and more. The colorful flecks of flower and leaves in the salad, the specks of color in the bread, and in the sauce did indeed make up a repast worthy of royalty, royalty such as Catherine de' Medici, the Poisoner of Paris.

I felt somewhat complicit, but they had, after all, come to this dinner party with murder on their minds. I was but the tool in their nefarious scheme. Nothing to do but slip away.

I slid around behind Celia. She sat still, as perhaps the enormity of what she had done dawned on her. I could only hope. My fingers itched for the feel of the scythe. What a relief it would be to be on my way, seeking the company of the gentle arachnids. The poisoner had placed the scythe next to her on the table. As I leaned in, her elbow accidentally nudged the tool out of easy reach.

She laughed again and forked a large bite of cake into her mouth. "Cancer."

The scythe was inches from my grasp. I extended my

arm. She jostled it farther away. "Nice touch, the spiders."

She was addressing me.

"The only thing they could hurt was a fly. They were just plain ordinary wolf spiders. What did you think they were? Brown recluse, right?" She waved her fork laden with cake in front of her face, then inserted the utensil into her mouth, and clicked the tines with her teeth. "It's the eyes. You have to pay attention to the eyes."

She turned toward me. I looked into the most terrifying eyes I'd ever seen.

"Now, what do I do with you?" she asked.

I was very, very glad that I was already dead.

Madcap Midwestern Mythologies
Brett Alan Sanders
The Boys That Just Refused to Die

Had me my first vision of those dadgum, ball-playing wizards when I was doing what the injuns call a vision quest, my great-grandpappy said one boiling hot summer's day. They was way down in their underworld, he told me, engaged in mortal combat with the skeleton gods that was ruling that place.

Only it weren't a real proper vision quest, since he weren't exactly all alone.

Ain't that right, Daddy Bones? Tell them you was right there with me, initiating your one-and-only male offspring in the ways of your injun ancestors.

Sure enough, right next to Gramps where he's been sitting and jawing there suddenly appears — out of the blue, it almost seems — that ancient old coot Napoleon Bonyparte Sanders. Slim as a skeleton, like one of those aforementioned lords of disease and gods of death.

Gramps give a poke to his daddy's skeleton ribs and the old Indian jumped awake. Mumbled something incoherent and smacked his lips against toothless gums near a gazillion times before nodding back off to his eternal sleep.

Vision quest proper or no, Gramps explains, facts is facts, and one of them facts is that Pops and me went up on a hill not far from these parts, and looking eastward and a little north went projecting our spirits towards the big serpent mounds over by *Cincinnatah*. And call me a liar, but I seen me one helluva vision.

Them mound-builders, I learnt me first of all, they was doing more'n just mound-building. Cause I seen me a ladder going down into the earth just right there alongside the tail end of the serpent mounds. A ladder going down to Hell, you might say, or down into Hades, or *Shebalba* (or *Hebalba*), whatchamacallit, don't make me no never-mind. A ladder going down to the underworld, anyhow, instead of like Jacob's ladder straight up into Heaven, where the angels was going up and down it connecting Jacob and his people to the Lord God of their father Abraham.

These mound-builders, anyways, was pretty much just like their distant cousins the pyramid-builders. Smack down there in Old Mexico, Gramps used to like saying. In that peninsular land they call *Yukeytan*, and locales further south. My visions, he says, weren't only a lot like the story of them Yukeytan injuns' sacred book *Papal Voodoo*, but they was the story's bedrock-solid source. According to what the messenger-angel told me, at least. And this weren't no angel of darkness, neither, take my word for it.

Gramps was off and running, then, with the subject of them so-called Hero Twins with their pitch-black rubber ball. Summoned down to that devils' kingdom for making so much racket right over their bony palace. Down through that Cross Roads between Earth Above and Land Below, which the Mayan Indians called Shebalba. Summoned to play against those old devils on their own demon court.

All in all, it's a purty good tale. I like, for instance, the part about how the Virgin Maria of Guadalupe gets herself kidnapped right out of Nazareth — or out of some hard-to-pronounce Mexican village, it might of been — by demons from mound-builder or pyramid-builder Hell. But then somehow she just gives them the slip. And the Hero Twins' skeleton father helps her escape all the way back up to earth. Only along the way he immaculately impregnates her by the magic semen he spits through his bony skull.

That father, though, clearly wasn't as wise as his heroic offspring. So's when the devious lords had long ago called him down to play the sacred ball game, the poor hapless blunderer right away got himself bamboozled plumb out of his flesh and blood.

But the part of the Hero Twins' saga that old Grandpappy most liked recalling, he says, is how those *mischeevious* clever boys went from playing some strange combination of hockey and soccer, by day (with the goal being a sideways stone ring on an outside wall in the temple complex), to by night getting thrown in the calaboose and put in ever new forms of mortal danger. And how those demon angels got all in a huff every morning them rascals come out of their traps undamaged goods.

"Dadgummit, but those boys just don't wanna die!" the skeleton lords would set themself to complaining.

But even when they finally do die, they're just sorta pretending. Or else maybe resurrecting. They stay further underground for a while, is all, and come back up like some old injun Houdinis, the angel showed me. Start chopping animals' limbs off their bodies and putting them back like they was. Hacking off each other's head and stuff, blood spurting up like hissin serpents, and then put the head back again like nothing ever happened. Sawing coffins in half, now, with each other inside, before pulling back the lids and bringing their already bled-and emptied-out brother back to life. Patching up the separated halves of the sawed-apart body with nary a scar.

Sorta like Humpty Dumpty, you know, except reversed and ever so much more bloody. They didn't need no Demon-gods' horses or Devil-lords' men to put themself back together again.

Finally those astoundingly boneheaded spooks got so excited by all this avant-garde performance art, they was practical salivating over the chance of getting themself in on it too. Only those boys that just refused to die? After cutting the vile old tyrants into pieces, they didn't much feel like bringing them back to life. And so they just kinda forgot to perform that part of the act.

That's how the Hero Twins redeemed their people from the clutches of eternal suffering and anguish. So's they too, when they make the inevitable journey down into that devilish underworld, from which no one never comes back, might outwit their evil overlords and achieve their heathen rest.

But the real moral of the story? In the right-now of this madcap, mystifying world we inhabit?

That's easy, old Grandpop shouts. Reaching out to us from across all the infinite time and space that separates us. Just wipe the goshdurn snot from your face, kid, and stop your whimpering and sniveling, he says. Toughen up like those godawful, obstinate, brave, marvelous-good boys, he says. And kick the dadblame devil in his man parts.

Ain't that what our own Good Book done been teaching us already?

Note: While the pronunciation is disputed, the name of the Maya underworld is spelled with an *X* and an *i*: *Xibalba*. The correct name of their sacred book is *Popol Vuh*, which is available to English readers in an excellent translation (from the original Quiché Maya) by Dennis Tedlock.

Me, Slap-Jim & The Right Reverend I. M. Devine
Ginny Fleming

So. There we was. . . . Wastin' away the night in a wooded-marshy piece of God's Country, somewhere 'tween Laconia and Gnaw-Bone, Indiana. Which if'n you knew your way 'round Indiana, you'd know they's 'bout a hunert' miles 'tween the two spits in the road. Ya see . . . I ain't 'bout to tell ya where I was. Naw. If I did, then I figure I'd have'ta kill ya — and seein' as how we just met. Well, Momma didn't raise no heathens. Least, none she knew of.

Me an' Slap-Jim was both sittin' in the dim light of the fire, whittlin' on walnut branches. Whittlin' nuthin' really. Just shavin' some twigs, as my grandpappy used to say. Slap-Jim — a big strappin', good natured colored man — never met a stranger 'less he didn't know ya. Jawin' like old friends do. Not sayin' nuthin'. Mostly grunts and snickers. That's how it is with old pals.

Slap-Jim an' me grew up together. We called him "Slap-Jim" cause if anything went wrong and one of our parents went lookin' for the guilty party — we'd all cry out: "Slap Jim! Slap 'im! Jim did it!" We was all happy-wicked chillins. Ever one of us needed the seat of our pants tanned on a regular basis. Our two ramshackled houses neighbored each other. I could'a lobbed a rock clean through the winder where Slap-Jim slept in a rumpled bed with his nest of brothers. Slap-Jim was the youngest son of eight — with a side order of four sisters. He bein' the baby of the family, as I was. Man. . . when ya got all us chillin' together. . . . Let's just say, we was a wild bunch a'heathens. Ahhh. . . . Weren't them the days.

So. There we was. Each of us sittin' on our special hacked an' carved log-stumps. Mine fit my butt like a glove an' I knew Slap-Jim was fond'a his as well. The warmth of our "enterprise" kept us toasty as we waited in the darkness for the glimmer of an oil lamp. We waited for the "Right Reverend I. M. Devine". Seriously. Ira Moses Devine.

The Rev didn't care much for Slap-Jim, though he always pretended with his butter-wouldn't-melt eyes up to God. But he pumped my hand ever' chance he got an' asked to be remembered to my ma. Momma would'a thrown that holy low-life out with the scummy bathwater an' then boxed *my* ears all the way to Heaven's Pearly Gates if she'd known I was fixin' to meet up with that lizard for Devil knows what in the dark o' night. But my Momma respected the office, if not the man. After all, he *did* have the word "Reverend" at the front of 'is name, an' all the scummy parts — like bein' a married man an' bein' over-fond of the "marital layin' on o'hands" — were all hear-say — *or so Momma claimed* — not worth the paper they was written on nor the gossip monger's dirty underwear.

So. There we was. Me an' Slap-Jim. In the dark. With just the light of the fire an' the sweet scent of our labor in the night air.

Suddenly, I spied a faint wobblin' glow off to the left o' camp. Maybe the good Rev was 'bout to grace us with his *divine* presence. We — me an' Slap-Jim — got to our feet, while silently resting our hands on our twin squirrel rifles. I sent the secret whistle through the gap in my front teeth an' waited to a count of three for the reply.

"Phwweet! Pheddle-Phwweet!"

Yeah. That's the ticket. Totally wrong response, though. Supposed to be the call of a barn owl, not a "twiddly-dee" bird. But the blasted fool always got it wrong. The good Rev had arrived. I looked at Slap-Jim an' grinned. He grinned back. Money good as in hand! In fact, I was already tastin' our "nuther good job done" steak dinner.

"Hello, boys! God is good, yes? Can I get me a big amen?"

"Amen," Slap-Jim muttered. He lowered his head to hide his goofy grin from the phweety-tweetin' preacher. "Yawser. . . . That be a *big* amen, Rev."

I hid my snickers 'hind a quick coughin' fit. Made like I caught my breath an' steepled my hands, raisin' pious eyes to Heaven above. "Oh — Amen, Rev. Aaaaa-Men!"

"Ahhh. . . . Cut the bull-cocky, Big John. It's been a coon's age" — an' this is where he sneered at Slap-Jim — "since you two even set foot inside the church. Ain't your mommas after both your asses 'bout your very souls?"

"Sorry, Reverend." I hung my head and tried my best 'ta look miserable. I counted to ten and shuffled my right foot, digging the toe of my boot into the dusty ground. My left hand gripped one of my coverall galluses. "Rev? We got a good run fer ya. Slap-Jim an' me cooked it up last night. Wanna lil' taste?" If I hadn't already known he did, the hungry look in his eyes would'a sold 'im out. He had the hunger. Had it *bad*.

His tongue made a hasty dash 'round his lips an' he stroked his widow maker goatee. "Now, son. . . ," he began an' his words trailed off.

I truly hated it when he called me son. He knew my pappy went to his Heavenly reward two years ago. But what he *didn't* know was — even before my pappy passed — I'd seen the lustful glances Reverend Devine gave my Momma ever' time she turned her back on 'im. 'Nother thing he didn't know was, three days after we'd laid Pa in his eternal resting place — unknown to my Momma — I was standin' in the broom closet when that slimy snake paid one'a his last bereavement calls to our house.

Tryin' to be quiet as a mouse, I was searchin' out Pa's secret recipe he wrote down and used to make the finest White Lightnin' in three counties. Earlier that summer, when he'd started feelin' poorly, Pa'd took me aside and made me take a solemn oath to continue his secret business. No one but his own partner — Slap-Jim's two-years-dead pappy — knew Pa was the county's ridge-runner. At least, none of the righteous church-goin' people knew. I promised Pa that me an' Slap-Jim would continue carin' for our own to the best of our abilities and I'd make him proud. An' I gave Slap-Jim's promise for 'im, too, since he wasn't there to do it. Then I went to my secret spot in the barn loft an' cried. Both from sadness for the kind'a man I knew I'd become and pride from Pappy havin' such powerful faith in his youngest pup.

So. . . . The good reverend didn't know there was a witness when my Momma slapped his cheek, sendin' him tumblin' to the floor. I reckon her pretty nails left their mark on his guilty face for a good forty-five minutes. He *didn't know* someone had overheard the vile, disgusting threats he hissed to my sainted momma while my pappy lay still fresh in his eternal grave. *Momma* didn't know either. I never mentioned it — Momma has her pride. I waited until I knew

XX SIW Goes **Platinum**

Momma had gone to bed before quietly lettin' myself out the door. It was a long night spent in the barn loft contemplatin'. Dawn came, an' I knew my path.

~*~

The word "son" had barely left the reverend's lips when I realized I'd clenched my right hand, digging my nails into my palm. "*Enough of that*," I silently told myself. "*Good things come . . . Good things. . . .*" I calmed myself an' forced a smile on my face, swallowin' bad memories from that long an' lonely night spent in that loft.

I watched as Slap-Jim handed the Rev a Ball jar of product, clear as spring water, from the left side corner of the opened up 'sample crate' we always left open to show our customers what they's spendin' their hard-earned money on. Then he reached down an' picked up a full jar o' hooch from the right side of the crate. Each container held thirty identical jars like the one in the good reverend's hand — an' the one Slap-Jim was fixin' to serve up. He wet the bottom of an empty jar with about a quarter cup's worth of sweet liquid fire. Slap-Jim handed me that very small swallow, poured two fingers for himself, then clinked jars with me an' tipped the clear firewater to his lips . . . brown, like caramel candy.

"Jus' a li'l taste of 'heaven'." I winked at Slap-Jim. He grinned back.

"Oooo. . . . My, my," Slap-Jim cooed. "That *shure* some fine, fine White Lightnin', Big John. You done outdid your ownself there. I do declare this the finest hootch we've ever cooked up. *Smooooth*. . . . But leaves a fire down below."

I threw all my drink to the back'a my throat, swallowed, an' immediately bent over an' grabbed my knees. The breath

117

left my throat with a hoarse death-rattle, an' I threw up one hand as if testifying'. "Sweet Je-susss. . . . *Ain't that smoooth?*"

Reverend Devine glanced back an' forth from Slap-Jim an' me an' then to the jar in his own hand. He licked dry lips once more, then grinned an' tipped his Lightnin' toward the full moon. He must'a had a powerful thirst, 'cause it seemed he couldn't drain his half-filled jar fast enough. He closed his eyes, swooned slightly an' I whispered to Slap-Jim so quiet only he could hear, wonderin' if'n I'd made *that* batch too powerful.

I mean, what if I killed that wicked "Man o' God", right here — right now? I began havin' visions of a dark night spent diggin' a grave that no stone cross would ever mark. But then, Reverend Devine rallied an' regained his balance.

"Mighty fine." He wheezed them words with a gaspin' breath. "Mighty . . . *Mighty fine.* Fit for the gold cups of Saints and Kings. I'm sure my *clients* will be happy with your *offering.* I declare — It is good with the Lord!"

I bit my tongue at 'is blasphemy an' fisted my hands, tryin' to keep my hatred of this miserable man outta my spoken words. "If you got the payment, Rev — Slap-Jim an' me'll load you up, all right?"

He did an' we did an' we (me an' Slap-Jim) were plum tuckered after loading those dang crates. But it was a good kind'a tired. We all shook hands afore the reverend drove off under the light of the full moon in his heavy-laden truck filled with crates of White Lightnin' covered an' muffled under a bed o' straw. The Rev was headed 'cross the river into Lou'avul, plannin' to sell his purchase to a secret speak-easy for a pretty penny. I silently wagered that the Right Reverend I. M. Devine wasn't known as a "Man o' the Cloth" down in Kentucky. I turned to Slap-Jim an' snickered. He laughed back.

"Wonder what those mob-boys'll think of the Rev's pretty jars of spring water?" Slap-Jim chuckled, handin' me a full jar of *real* Lightnin' this time. He took his own an' sat down on his butt-worn stump, raised his water-clear glass in a toast an' said: "Here's to your momma, Big John."

There we was. . . . I smiled an' raised my drink to the sky — jus' watchin' the hooch swirl in the silvery moonlight shinin' through that Ball jar.

I silently nodded an' grinned. "Way I figure it, Slap-Jim. . . . Them mob-boys? They just might'a saved me from diggin' an unmarked grave tonight."

Double Digging
Andrea Gilbey

"Does anyone have any more to add to the minutes?" Myrna peered over her half-moon glasses and glanced around the table.

Debbie shook her head and drew a wriggly line under the last note on her pad, ending the line with a scribbled rose. Other heads shook around the table and a few voices muttered, "No," or "Nothing from me." A tuneless rhythmic breathy noise came from the seat on Debbie's left as her neighbour whistled silently through the gap in his teeth.

Myrna swept her gaze around the table once more, studiously avoiding eye contact with Malcolm, who was well known for being pedantic about points of order, and had once tried to waste a whole meeting in a debate about whether Myrna should be addressed as "Madam Chairman", "Madam Chairwoman" or just plain "Chair." On that occasion the lady in question had put a firm end to the discussion in her no-nonsense style.

"I'm not a man, last time I looked, I'm not a piece of furniture, I'm not a madam, and this is not the House of Commons. My name is Myrna, please call me by it."

Myrna signed her name at the bottom of the minutes sheet with a flourish, capped her fountain pen and pushed her papers to one side.

"Now, questions and tips. Who wants to start? Kaz?"

One of the society's newer members lowered the hand she had tentatively raised and smiled. Debbie instinctively smiled back; she liked Kaz a lot. The girl's bleached blonde dreadlocks, nose ring and peace sign tattoos had caused some sniffiness among a few of the older members, but by sheer force of personality Kaz had won over the doubters, and was turning into a good gardener. Her immaculate allotment held neat rows of organically grown vegetables, though how she found the time to keep it so tidy while holding down a full time job and looking after her seven year old son was anyone's guess.

"I'm sure this is a real newbie question," she apologised, "but I'm having awful problems with black fly on my broad beans. Any ideas, please?"

A buzz of conversation started up around the table as all the members tried to put forward their own personal solution. Debbie turned to the silent man beside her.

"Steve, didn't you tell us you had won several classes with your broad beans?" she asked loudly enough to be heard over the babble. "How did you manage the black fly?"

Her neighbour flipped a lock of dark blond floppy hair away from his face and smiled a disarming smile, showing the gap in his teeth. As always, Debbie felt irritated at herself for finding *him* irritating. She secretly harboured an idea that the second newest member of the group thought himself endearing and adorable and was quite convinced that everyone else agreed with him.

"Well, I . . . I suppose it must have been the climate, or the area or something, but I didn't get black fly. Maybe I'm just lucky, hmm?" he winked chummily at Kaz, who stared stony faced back at him for a frozen second, one eyebrow raised, then turned to the elderly man beside her. Debbie watched the girl's reaction interestedly. So she wasn't the only one who found him annoying.

"So Dave, you think that will work?" Kaz was saying to the older man loudly. Dave adjusted his hearing aid with a piercing whistle and repeated the advice that he, and most of the rest of the group, had already given.

"I say weak soapy water, sprayed on them three times a day." He nodded sagely. Corner-wise across the table from him and slightly out of his eye line Babs grinned at Debbie and rolled her eyes.

"The oracle has spoken." Babs said in a stage whisper that Dave's hearing aid would never catch.

Myrna cleared her throat to call the assembly together again.

"Any more questions?" The heads shook again. "Then any hints or tips, anyone?" She saw by Dave's quizzical expression that he hadn't heard what she said. "Any tips?" she bawled.

"Buy new batteries," Steve sniggered. Debbie kicked him under the table.

"I've been working on a new tomato feed," announced Dave, "and I think I've found a really good recipe."

Pens were clicked all around the table as the members prepared to take down words of wisdom from their most experienced colleague. Steve shot his cuffs and sat up looking intent and Malcolm started a fresh page of his notebook, dating the page and writing in neat block capitals, "Dave's Tomato Feed" before ruling a double line under the words.

Dave proceeded to ramble his way through a recipe involving boiled nettles, alfafa tablets, borage leaves, egg shells and cat hair while his friends made copious notes.

"And of course there's one special ingredient," he finished, winking and tapping the side of his nose. "It mustn't go any further than this room." He looked dramatically over his shoulders, right, then left, until Myrna's steely glare caught his eye. The group leader tapped her watch pointedly.

"It'll be poo," Babs muttered under her breath, "it's always poo."

Debbie stifled a giggle as Dave declaimed, "Rabbit . . . poo." He glanced in turn at Myrna, Debbie, Kaz and Babs with a slight old-fashioned bow before uttering the second word. Debbie wasn't sure whether to be flattered that he thought her enough of a lady to be protected from four letter words, or offended that he thought her too uptight to know them.

There being no more tips or ideas forthcoming, Myrna turned the subject to the upcoming Inter-Club produce show between the Fairbrook Horticultural Society and their main rivals, the society from the neighbouring village of Harpers Green.

"As we all know; Harpers Green have won the show cup for the last two years. Ted Buckland is determined to make it a hat trick this year, so we need to pull out something really special to get Fairbrook's name back on the cup. Divide and rule should be our strategy. We need as many entries in as many different classes as possible to stand a chance of winning the show trophy. I will be entering five classes, a Plate of Five Runner Beans, a Plate of Onions From Sets, a Basket of Kitchen Vegetables, a Plate of Tomatoes and the Heaviest Onion."

As she spoke she handed round lists of the available classes for entry.

"Whew!" Kaz puffed out her cheeks. "Five runner beans? Just five? There's no room for error there, is there!"

"Perfection is the only way to win," beamed Babs, running her eyes eagerly over the list. "I'll be entering my tomatoes as usual, and I'm hoping to have a nice crop of early whites this year, aaaannnd . . . shallots." She smiled around the table, already seeing her perfect vegetables lying smugly on a black velvet cloth.

"I will be entering my onions, as usual, in the Three Identical Onions class, and if my carrots are as good as last year I should be able to do well in the One Carrot No Shorter Than Seven Inches class," said Malcolm, writing his choices in his notebook in precise capitals and proceeding to draw a planting plan on a new blank page.

"Spuds for me," beamed Dave, "All the classes! And tomatoes," a dirt-ingrained finger ran down the list. "And I might have a punt at the Vase of Sweet Peas this year."

A respectful hush settled on the table. Ted Buckland was famous throughout the district for his tomatoes and sweet peas, so Dave's challenge would not go unnoticed, and should he win it would be a great coup for the Fairbrook Society.

"I need to take this home and talk to Stuart when he gets back from his parent teacher evening. I can't make any decisions without my head gardener," smiled Debbie, waving the list and tucking it into her notebook. "What about you, Steve? Which classes will you enter?"

"Oh, I don't know. . . ," he pouted and flicked his hair. I've won pretty much all of these classes in the past so it's a hard decision." He gave the room the benefit of his gap-toothed smile. "I'll let you know." He shuffled his papers together and stood up.

Myrna, reclaiming her authority, stood up and collected her floral shopping bag.

"If we're all done then I'll see you next week at the same time. Goodnight, everyone."

Driving home from work the next evening, Debbie's eye was caught by a tall figure with floppy hair, standing by the side of the road talking to someone. She tooted her horn and flapped a hand out of the window with a smile, but when she looked in her rear view mirror the smile changed to a puzzled expression. The young man was talking animatedly to Ted Buckland, and in his hand was his notebook, the same notebook he had been writing in last night. She recognised the childish Batman cover. The two men were bending over the page, following the tip of Steve's pen as he pointed to a line in the book and neither looked up at her toot.

"Hello, anyone home?" She threw her bag onto the kitchen table, making a draught that blew a piece of lined paper to the floor. Woodstock scuttled under the table after it and Debbie deftly scooped it away from the dog's claws as she walked to the sink to fill the kettle. While she waited for it to boil she read in Stuart's slanting scrawl, "Sorry Debs, I'll be late tonight, I forgot it's year nine parents' evening. Don't wait dinner if you're hungry. Love you."

She wasn't particularly hungry and after finishing her tea she looped Woodstock's lead from the coat rack and looked at him encouragingly.

The evening air was just a little chilly as the pair strode out across the downs. Woodstock romped on ahead, chasing rabbits, unaware that his frantic barking was giving them at least a five-minute warning to get away. Debbie balled her fists in the deep, baggy pockets of her aran cardigan, threw back her head and took a deep lung full of the clear air.

Woodstock came gambolling back, barking, running around her in a tight circle and haring away again up the hill.

"What is it, boy, what are you showing me?" she panted as she followed him up the slope.

The dog was running towards a bent figure, who seemed to be scouring the ground for something.

"Hello! Lost a contact lens?" she called cheerily. "The times that's happened to me. . . ."

She stopped in confusion as the figure straightened up. It was Ted Buckland, his face flushed from stooping and embarrassment.

"Oh, hi, Debbie. I won't shake hands, I'm collecting, er. . . ," he indicated the polythene bag in his left hand.

Rabbit droppings? The image of this man and her gardening colleague standing head to head over a notebook flashed into her head. Dave's recipe! The slimeball had shared Dave's tomato feed recipe with the rival club's chairman! Just wait till she got her hands on that little. . . .

Clenching her fists she forced a smile.

"Each to their own," she laughed gaily. "Come on Woodstock, here boy." She dug a tennis ball from her pocket and hurled it down the hill, running down after the excitable dog so fast that she almost tripped.

~*~

"So what do you think I should do?" she finished, through the last mouthful of garlic bread.

"Are you sure Steve was reading from his FHC notebook?" asked Stuart.

"Positive. It's weird enough that a grown man uses a child's Batman exercise book, why would he have two the same? I don't want to tell Myrna yet, I don't have any real proof, and you know how she worries about the slightest conflict in the group. I'll sleep on it and maybe talk to Babs tomorrow. There's plenty of time before next week's meeting."

Stuart nodded.

"Good idea. Babs has been in the society even longer than we have, she'll know how to handle this. I'll make sure I get away in time to come to the next meeting to see what this chap's up to."

~*~

After selling large letter stamps to someone who wanted second class regular letter stamps, sticking a Special Delivery label on upside down, and almost giving a holiday-maker dollars instead of Euros, Debbie realised that her mind wasn't on her job. In her head she was having imaginary confrontational conversations with Steve even though as yet she had no proof that anything underhand was going on. She frowned and tapped her nails on the counter as her last customer left the shop. Was it just that she instinctively didn't like the man? No, he was up to something, sure as eggs are. . . .

Eggs!

The doormat buzzer rudely interrupted her thoughts and she pulled herself together enough to check a passport form thoroughly, but once the customer left she let her thoughts go back to the trail of eggs. 4.30, the postman would be in to collect the day's mail in a few minutes and she could close the post office counter. If no-one came in for any groceries before the postman came she could maybe close up early. . . . She nodded, answering her own unspoken question and picked up the phone.

"Fairbrook Library, Yvonne speaking, how may I help?"

"Vonnie, it's me, have you got time to dig something out of the local rag archives before you close?"

"Debs, you sound quite breathless! What's the matter?"

"Oh, something and nothing, maybe, gardening club stuff, but I'm working on a hunch here, humour me, please. Would you be able to find the news reports on the Inter Club show from '99? If you can hunt them out before closing time I'll pop over as soon as I can, I think I know what I'm looking for."

"1999?" queried Yvonne, "Isn't that the year of the Great Egg Disaster? Are you sure you want to look back at that?"

"Yes," said Debbie firmly, "Can you find it?"

"Shouldn't take more than ten minutes," affirmed Yvonne.

"Good, I'll be over as soon as I've locked up."

Quickly, before another customer had a chance to open the door, she flipped the sign to "closed" and hurried through to the back office to make everything secure for the night. The red post van pulled up as she opened the front door to leave, and she bundled the post bags into the collection driver's arms, barely allowing him time to scan the collection point bar code.

"What's your hurry, Debbie, got a hot date?" the man grinned.

She ignored the comment and pushed him away from the door so she could bring down the shutter.

"See you tomorrow, Wayne."

~*~

The newspapers she had asked for were laid out neatly on a table in the study area of the library, and Yvonne was waiting, curious to know what the urgency was.

Debbie dropped her bag beside a chair and started leafing through the papers before she even greeted her friend.

"Vonnie, you're an angel, well done. Now then . . . no, not this one, must be in the Gazette. . . ."

She flipped pages, licking her finger to get a grip on the paper.

"Here!"

She stabbed at the page, pointing to a headline in large type above a photo of a man and a boy holding a trophy. "Eggstravaganza At Local Flower Show," the headline read.

Debbie stared at the photo. There was Ted Buckland, younger, slimmer and with more hair, and holding the other handle of the large silver cup he was grasping was a small boy with floppy blond hair and a gap between his front teeth.

Debbie read the article aloud, gabbling so fast that Yvonne could only catch one word in three, so she moved round to read over her friend's shoulder.

"Local grower Ted Buckland poses with the Inter-Club cup, assisted by his nephew, ten year old Stephen Peet. Buckland's best in show for his vase of spectacular sweet peas helped secure the club trophy for the Harper's Green Horticultural Society. The event was not without drama, as an accident involving prime clutch of goose eggs, entered by local post mistress Debbie Clark from the Fairbrook H.S., turned a close run competition into a triumph for the visiting club."

"That's him!" exclaimed Debbie, "The kid who knocked the trestle table over and smashed all my eggs. I swear he did it on purpose, and he's still at it!"

"Have you been out weeding in the full sun again, Debs?" Yvonne's expression was bemused. "Who's still at what?"

Debbie stabbed again at the photo, poking the face of

the grinning boy.

"Him. He's in our club, joined a few months ago. He reckons he's won cups and rosettes for just about anything you can grow, but he's living in a flat, allegedly borrowing a friend's garden, and has never once produced any evidence of anything he's grown, or even the slightest bit of dirt under his nails. The other day I caught him showing his club notes to Ted Buckland. His *uncle*."

"So you think he's a mole? Gardening . . . mole . . . geddit?" Yvonne nudged her.

Debbie rolled her eyes.

"Very funny." She nibbled at her nails, thinking fast.

"Can I take a copy of this? I need to talk to some of the other club members. This . . . man . . . could completely sabotage our chances in the inter club show."

Yvonne was already spreading the page on the glass of the photocopier.

"This is on the house," she said, as Debbie rummaged in her purse for a twenty pence piece to pay for the copy. "It'll be worth it if the Egg Smasher finally gets his comeuppance."

~*~

"Here they come." Babs nudged Dave and woke him up from an after dinner snooze. Kaz jumped up from her deckchair and ushered Debbie into it, turning it slightly so the older woman was shaded by Dave's rows of runner bean plants. Stuart nodded to the other club members and perched on a large upturned flowerpot. They'd decided to meet on Dave's allotment as it was quiet and they would hear anyone approaching, not that Debbie could now imagine that Steve had ever set foot on an allotment.

Babs handed Debbie a glass of her peapod wine and

offered a plate of chocolate chip cookies.

"So come on then, spill the beans, why all the secrecy?"

Debbie unfolded the photocopy and held it out to the others. She pointed to the boy in the picture.

"Recognise him?"

She told the story, starting with the saga of the smashed goose eggs for Kaz's benefit, and finishing with her sighting of Steve passing Dave's recipe to his uncle.

Kaz's eyes flashed and she balled her fists.

"He's a spy! Kick him out of the club!"

"We've no proof, Kaz," came the voice of reason from Stuart. "That's why we don't want to tell Myrna yet, she'll only worry. We need to watch him. He'll trip himself up sooner or later, that type always does."

"I've got a better idea," said Babs, grinning, "Let's set him up. Feed him something he can pass on, but make sure Harpers Green won't benefit from it."

Three faces lit up with delight at her suggestion. Dave looked from one to the other of them, as they all turned and smiled at him.

"Dave, get your recipe book out, let's see what we can come up with."

~*~

"Any hints and tips?" asked Myrna. "The big day is only three weeks away, so the more knowledge we can share the better we will do as a team." She beamed round the table at the members, encouraged by their reports of blooming plants and flourishing vegetables. She was confident that her own basket of kitchen vegetables would be a veritable cornucopia of deliciousness, she had so much produce coming to ripeness.

"I've worked on an improvement to my tomato feed."

Dave pulled a sheaf of papers from a tatty carrier bag. "To save you all having to write it out again, Debbie's very kindly typed it out for me."

He peeled a sheet from the top of the pile, peered at the hand-written name on the top and passed it to Malcolm.

Debbie and Babs carefully avoided looking at each other or catching Kaz's eye. Typing the recipe and giving out individually named copies was Kaz's idea — with Malcolm and Myrna not in on the plot it was the only way the bogus recipe could be fed to Steve without innocent parties using it by mistake. The three women and Stuart had carefully positioned themselves around the table so that there was no chance of Myrna or Malcolm catching a glimpse of Steve's copy and realising that it was different from theirs.

"Hmm, very interesting!" Steve studied the sheet of paper, nodding wisely. "I shall make sure I mix some up as soon as I get home, although my tomatoes really don't need it. They're turning into real beauties."

"I'll pop round tomorrow night and have a look at them," said Dave, "You're using your friend's garden down Brook Street, aren't you? Third house in from the top?"

"Er, yes, yes, I am," Steve stuttered, "but, um, it might not be convenient . . . er. . . ."

"It's ok, you don't have to wait in, I'll go along the back alley and peek over the fence," beamed Dave. "It's no trouble."

Steve smiled weakly.

~*~

"That's four fifty two, please love . . . oh, sorry, one moment . . . Fairbrook Post Office, Debbie speaking."

An excited voice hissed urgently in her ear.

"Debs he's here, the Egg Smasher, using the photocopier!"

It was Yvonne.

"Can you see what he's copying?" asked Debbie.

"No, but the copier's low on paper, and I deliberately didn't fill it. If he makes more than a few copies it'll stop and he'll have to call me over."

"Genius!" gloated Debbie. "Call me back in a bit." She waved her customer out and fidgeted at the counter, arranging and re-arranging gift cards, not wanting to move away from the phone. Her hand shot out to grab it at the first ring.

"Well?"

"It says "'Dave's Tomato Feed — Revised Recipe,'" hissed Yvonne.

"Gotcha!" Debbie punched the air.

Stuart suddenly straightened up from loading the dishwasher.

"Oh, Debs, I've got something to show you," he pulled his phone from his pocket and swiped the screen. "I popped into the garden centre after school to get some cane toppers before you poke your eye out on those broad bean poles, and you'll never guess who I saw skulking around with a trolley full of tomato plants."

He handed the phone to his wife.

"Swipe through the gallery, there's a few. I had to zoom in from a distance so he didn't see me, but you can see who it is. More evidence."

Debbie nodded and smiled gleefully at her husband.

"And what do you bet he won't have the brains to take the labels off before Dave gets round there on his visit."

They hi-fived each other, laughing.

~*~

Myrna walked back to her place flushed and beaming

and fluttered her first place ribbon at her club colleagues.

"Well done, Myrna," Debbie patted her leader's shoulder, "that basket is beautiful."

"It's neck and neck," said Myrna, "It's all down to the tomato classes and the Best in Show, and I think that's between your goose eggs and Malcolm's onions."

The group quietened as the judge approached the tomato tables. Every plate was heaped with glowing red fruit, and there was very little to choose between them in appearance.

"Good colour, nice and firm, and they smell. . . ." the judge raised the plate to his nose and smiled, "wonderful!"

He cut the topmost fruit in half and the small crowd craned forward to see.

"Good firm flesh, nice thin skin, plenty of seeds, let's taste. . . . Mmm! Sweet and juicy, very good."

He moved along the table, cutting and tasting one fruit from each plate. The last plate on the Fairbrook table was Steve's. The judge commented on the glowing colour, shining skin and firm feel of the fruit, then cut into one.

"Oh dear. Oh dear me, that's the worst case of blossom end rot I've ever seen. What a pity."

Debbie tried to keep her expression disappointed as she viewed the completely black insides of Steve's tomatoes. A gasp ran around the hall, and Ted Buckland took an involuntary step forward, glaring at the younger man, before he remembered that he wasn't supposed to know him, and stepped back, trying to look pleased that the rival club had done badly.

The judge moved to the Harper's Green table and started to examine the fruit. Every plate met with praise for its external appearance, but every fruit was black inside.

Almost as black as Ted Buckland's angry face. His club members gathered around in surprise and anger, and voices were raised inside the huddle. Ted's head lifted and his suffused face looked around for his errant nephew, but the young man had gone without waiting to hear the final result.

The judge cleared his throat.

"Well, um, I think it's quite clear from that round that the winner of all the tomato classes is the Fairbrook society. Very well done, and commiserations, Harper's Green. Now for the final result, although from the scores I can see that we already have a champion club."

He stepped back to the judging table and lifted the Best in Show shield.

"It was a very close run thing, but the winner of this year's Best in Show is . . . the goose eggs."

A piercing two-fingered whistle rang out from the crowd at the back of the hall as Debbie stepped out to collect her trophy, waving it in salute to Yvonne, who let fly another shrill celebration.

"And the overall Inter-Club trophy goes to. . . ," the judge raised his voice over the hubbub, "Fairbrook Horticultural Society."

"Where did Steve go?" asked a bemused Myrna, as her club-mates pushed her forwards to claim the cup.

"Don't worry about him," laughed Debbie, "I don't think we'll be seeing him again — he's gone, sure as eggs are eggs."

Madcap Midwestern Mythologies
Brett Alan Sanders

Don Quicksote's New Adventure of the Windmills

When Señor Donald Quicksote showed up one summer day at the county's spanking new consolidated high school, looking to teach some Spanish, my grandmom was one of the first in line to try out the new language. It was either that or another torturous year of French with Mamselle Florence B. *Floburt*. Who was more'n a bit touched in the head.

On top of that, Grandmom says, Miss Floburt had a decisive hysterical streak. She was known, behind her back, as "Flo Grizzly Burt," but when provoked she made a noise more like the mythical Loony Bird's powerful screeching.

Some of us incorrigible brats, when we found out her middle initial stood for *Bovary*, took to calling her "Flovary the Ovary Burt."

We wasn't always the sweetest of kids.

Quicksote, on the other hand, was what you might call an unknown quantity. As it turned out he proved mostly good-natured, easy-tempered, and respectful of the potentialities he claimed to see in the noble little savages swarming into and all over his classroom.

More important, he was easy to get off topic. All you had to do was start asking questions about *The Adventures of Donkey Hotee day La Mancha*. That was his favorite of all books. The true biography of some madman who was always mixing up windmills with giants. Wrote by some ancient Spanish guy name of *Sir Meegwell Vantees*, or simply: Sir Vantees.

Basically, or so he claims, he's a blood descendant of the real *Quix*otee clan. *Quicks*ote being, in fact, no more'n the British version of that distinguished Spanish surname. His branch of the family, though never big, come over thisaway in time for the *bloody American Rebellion* against good old King Georgie. Who come to be no less a lunatic than their ancestor, but a good deal less pleasant or exemplary company.

We learnt mighty fast that our own Quicksote had some bats in his belfry, too, but they wasn't of the sort (like Mamselle Ovary's) that made you wanna run for the hills.

Maybe the first clue that his toony-looniness was more'n just what some oldtimers call *queerness* — or *eccentricity*, as more polite folk would say — come when he was explaining, to some beginner class or other, the story of his ancestor the knight in rusted armor. Long story short, leaning against a table and whittling away at a piece of wood he was making into a walking stick (he was getting kind of old, after all, white hair and pointy beard, cricks in the bones and all), he come to the part in the adventure where Donkey Hotee's fixing to save his poor neighbors from what he took as an army of miscreant giants. Señor Quicksote's voice getting louder and more excited every second. Then all of a sudden he starts running like the dickens, in a sort of slow motion canter, down the center aisle, dumfounded innocents right and left of him. Stick pointed out in front like Sir Galahad's lance in some jousting party in jolly old England. Tilting, as the old expression has it, at the windmill piñata he'd hung up there his very self. And still hanging there like he'd left it. Dangling by a bit of string, tied up like a shoelace.

He charged ahead, anyways, after that poor inoffensive *paper-mahshay* windmill. Then play-acted being struck by one of its thrashing wooden arms, and falling down on his back. A couple of burly young students helped him up and he seemed his old self again, no Madder'n the next Hatter. Laughed it off with the class like it was just a game to get our attention. Plant the story in our heads with the force of an oldfangled projector in a darkened movie house.

The main adventure I'm getting at, anyways, come long ago one fateful summer while we was all out on vacation. Señor Quicksote didn't come back in the fall and rumors was flying as to why. Everyone and her cousin had a first-hand account and all of them contradicted one another. But I found out the truth one day in my English classroom, searching the Web for ideas for some world-mythology creative-writing assignment our teacher was torturing us with.

As it happens, I come upon a story from an old-style newspaper column, by the editor *maritis* or something like that. Which I guess means "has-been" or "used-to-of-been," and "who's as old as the hills" or "older'n dirt," judging from the picture beside his name (which I forget). And so they still let him write his little article once a week or once a month.

The paper's from a small town in the flatlands somewheres between Indianapolis and Topeka, anyways. I read the story two or three times through, rubbing my eyes to make sure I wasn't hallucinating, and then the bell ending class rang and I ain't been able to find it since. But I still remember it real good.

Either he's plumb out of his mind, says the "Howdy-

Neighbor" author, or he just seen him the living reincarnation of Donkey Hotee from the plains of La Mancha, somewheres over yonder in Spain. Who was always fighting evildoers and for their penance making them plant flowers day and night in the infinite garden of his sweet love Dulcet Nayuh. All of those labors being part-n-parcel of that knight-in-rusted-armor's knightly-errands.

How it happened that he seen the airy knight is he was making a tour of that sleek new wind farm out east of town. When suddenly the energy company's man who was taking him around, explaining how everything worked and all, let out a shriek and just skedaddled out of there. Ducking and covering like it was the Zombie Apocalypse. Looking behind him, then, old Howdy-Neighbor seen a rusty pick-up closing in at about two or three hundred miles an hour. And leaning out of the driver's window, sitting on the edge and aiming a semi-automatic pistol out ahead of him, was this gangly scarecrow of a man in blue jeans and gray t-shirt, white-haired and pointy-bearded like Sir Vantes and his Mad Knight rolled into one.

Now I seen all at once who it was, he says. And I seen what it was he was after. He must of took those wonders of modern technology to be some new, never-before-thought-of marauding giants. Not understanding that they was really our friends, gonna help save us (along with solar panels on all our rooftops) from the global warming. And though he couldn't make them out for sure over all the noise, he figured he could purty well guess, having read the book of his former adventures once or twice, at least the general nature of all the threats and oaths and insults he was nonstop hurling at whoever or whatever he was chasing.

And all the while some hapless farmer in bib overalls,

down-to-earth Saunchus Paunchus with his hairy chest and rounded belly, is reaching desperate across from the passenger seat trying to grab the wheel and get a foot on the brakes and keep his mentally-deranged or delusional or just impossible-dreaming companion from running the truck smack-dab into all that "titanium and steel," as I remember our impassioned scribbler calling it.

After that it's all a blur of tired old Rosy-Nanty, his metal horse, and police cars with sirens blaring and SWAT teams trailing behind with all the force of Homeland Security, and some distant fire and smoke where our unlucky pair apparently did run themself up against one of those newfangled windmill-giants of our hero's fancy.

Afterwards, rather than gawking like some crass looker-on at someone else's misfortune, the grizzled old reporter returned sorrowful to his own Rosy-Nanty of an antique word-processing machine to type up what we've just been hearing. Without the heart to go digging into whether the presumed knight and squire was alive or dead, knowing some younger and spryer reporter would take care of that unpleasant duty. Still not sure if he weren't dreaming it all, anyways. Or else what devilment had brung knight and squire to this Cruel Cross Roads with Death and Glory?

As for me, your crazy-demented prattler Madeline Sanders Polk, I never doubted for a second it was our old teacher. Finally gone and lost whatever thread of sanity it was had kept him going so long in this infernal Funny Farm we call the Civilized World.

A Tree Grows in Albuquerque

T. Lee Harris

"There we were! Me and the Chief up to our asses in pissed-off, walking broccoli!"

Across the crowded bar, in a booth behind a partition, Devlyn Frost resisted the urge to bury his face in his hands. Russ was at it again. Frost didn't get it. RSS104 was a synthoid so why in hell did he persist in telling tall tales in bars? Certainly not to cadge free drinks. Synthoids didn't take in liquids like that. Maybe it was something in his embedded personality. And why *that* story? Why Gaeans?

An involuntary shudder sloshed some of his drink into his lap. He took a quick steadying gulp and placed the glass back onto the scarred tabletop a bit too firmly. *Get a grip, you idiot.* Yeah. Right. That was way easier to say than to do. Gaeans. More properly, the Nova Terrans — Russ' pissed-off, walking broccoli — scared Frost on a primal level. One that reason couldn't easily dent.

The Gaea Wars had happened more than a century before, but, even as a schoolboy, he'd had a visceral reaction to the story of Gail Honigbaum and her Nova Terra movement. It went way beyond the horror of a boy sitting in a darkened classroom watching history vids of the former geneticist, by then renamed Gaea, leading rank after rank of genetically re-engineered followers against the human race. It went even beyond the shock of seeing lush forests consume neighborhoods that looked like his own in a matter of hours, or towns and cities in a matter of days.

Maybe it all boiled down to his inability to understand why someone would reject humanity to such an extent they'd voluntarily turn themselves into something more plant or insect than animal. Anger? He understood that. He had a fair whack of mad-at-the-world himself. And yeah, some humans could be treacherous bastards. He'd met more than his fair share of those, too, but to go *that* far?

The dull metal case resting in the shadows by his feet took on a palpable presence. Gaeans were the whole reason he and Russ were in the ABQ region in the first place. Some weeks back a scientist named Bolle with a group called NewMex Botanical Research hired them to go to the edges of one of the central Nova Terran strongholds to collect tissue samples. The man had been extremely nervous and the amount he'd offered was far too high. Frost and Russ had wondered at it, but the half payment the man presented in hard credit bars made a convincing argument. Besides, there wasn't anything illegal about collecting Nova Terran tissue. It was simply dangerous for a non-Gaean to venture into a so-called Eden. They'd barely escaped with their skins intact, but they'd gotten the material.

Russ's audience broke into a hearty laugh. Frost winced and slid farther down in the booth. He wasn't certain what had been said, but it was probably humiliating. It usually was. He checked the time again. If they were to meet Dr. Bolle, they needed to leave soon. Sounded like Russ was winding down, anyway. Probably keeping track of the time, too. The synthoid's internal timer was scary accurate — when he decided to pay attention to it.

XX SIW Goes Platinum

~*~

NewMex Botanical Research turned out to be a run-down cluster of buildings sprawled across the scrubby Sandia foothills like the stomped-on remains of a giant lizard. RSS104 stepped out of the still-idling skimmer and regarded the badly-lit area with skepticism. "Y'know, Chief, if there wasn't a big sign on that building, I'd swear the sat-nav dropped us at the wrong address."

"I hate when you call me that. Makes me feel like I should have gold braid on my shoulders or something. What's wrong with just Dev?" Frost pulled the metal case out of the back and joined his friend outside. "Hmmm. Got a point about the facility, though. Does look kinda well-used."

"Sorta like the rides. All two of them."

The vehicles in question were older road cars with no lift capabilities and both so dusty it was impossible to tell what color they were in the fading evening light. One of the cars was plastered with stickers bearing clever slogans such as "Botanists do it with flowers" and "Geneticists add splice to life". The back seat of the other was filled with junk, mainly old electronic parts and fast food containers.

"He said 'after hours meeting', Russ. That usually means the shop is closed and everyone else went home."

Russ still didn't move. "You never did ask Dr. Bolle why he wanted slices of tree guys to play with."

"Nope. I noticed you didn't, either. Come on. Let's finish this job and get the rest of our money. I don't know about you, but I'll be damned glad to get this Gaean crap far, far away from me."

They were a short distance from the building when a side door opened, spilling interior light across the gravel and backlighting the bulky figure of Dr. Bolle. "Gentlemen! You're right on time," he called. "I admire punctuality. Come in. The upstairs stasis unit awaits!"

The interior of the complex wasn't in any better shape than the exterior. It hadn't been too impressive to begin with, metal framing with cheap drywall partitions, built more for utility than beauty. Someone had slapped fresh paint onto a few of the aging metal door facings, but no effort had been made to remove the rust first, resulting in an uneven, pebbly surface that was already peeling in spots. A hodgepodge of posters were tacked along the hallway: nature shots, pictures of mountains with inspiring slogans, adverts for musical groups, all most likely marking the personal tastes of the denizens of the offices and labs beyond the drywall. The elevator was less than confidence-inspiring, too. Bolle prattled nervously over the creaks, groans, and rattles the entire ride to the second floor.

The lab he led them to was in sharp contrast to the rest of the place. A new, steel door with hardened locks opened onto a large room filled with new equipment and gleaming work surfaces. To one side, a wide rolling overhead door, the sort seen in warehouses, had been installed. Gone was the flimsy wallboard from downstairs. In its place was new, hardened fiberboard, painted a fresh white. The most prominent feature, was a massive, reinforced glass containment area that took up an entire corner of the room next to floor-to-ceiling shelves lined with featureless containers plastered with day-glo warning labels behind padlocked steel mesh shutters.

Frost swung the case onto the nearest table. "Here ya go, Doc. I think you'll be pleased. We got a pretty wide range of samples."

Dr. Bolle's fingers danced across the embedded keypad

until a band along the top went green and a large amount of text that seemed to consist of more numbers than letters slid past. The researcher beamed. "Excellent work, gentlemen! You even got some insectoid tissue! More than I dared hope!"

Yeah. The insectoid tissue. On their last collection run into the northern Wyoming Eden, a swarm of Nova Terran pollinators had found them. Russ flattened the leading edge of the swarm with a shovel. The rest reversed course and buzzed back in the direction they'd come. Frost and the synthoid had just enough time to collect the smashed bugs and dive into the skimmer before the swarm returned. With reinforcements. Between the clouds of toxic pollen and volleys of flying thorns, the mag-lift had barely gotten them off the ground.

Aloud, Frost said, "Well, you never said plant-form only and the opportunity presented itself."

"I am constantly amazed at the resourcefulness of you adventurers," Bolle said as the case slipped into a slot in the front of a massive stasis unit. With a slight hiss, the slot sealed after it so seamlessly, it was barely traceable except for the small light in the upper right corner that went from blinking yellow to solid green. Most of the slots had the solid green indicator.

"Actually, we prefer the term Salvage Specialists," Russ said with a broad grin.

"Regardless, you've more than earned your pay," the researcher said, opening a drawer and pushing several stacks of thin metal bars bound in bank wrappers across the table. "Hard credits just as you requested. I wasn't certain what values would be preferred so I got some of everything; from platinum to copper. Is that acceptable?"

Frost did a quick count and swept the bars into a bag that he tossed to Russ. "Yep," he said. "They all spend the same."

"I'll never understand why you adventurers — excuse me — *Salvage Specialists* always insist on hard credits," Dr. Bolle said as he escorted them back to the elevator. His previous nervousness was gone and he had now graduated to effusive. "Seems to me they're a damn sight harder to use than a digital credit transfer. Harder to obtain, too. I had to actually go all the way into Albuquerque to an actual physical bank. Been years since I did that."

Frost pressed the elevator button and said, "Hard credits take up a bit more room, I grant you, but sometimes we're not all that close to a bank."

"Or even cities," the synthoid added.

"Truth to tell, I'm glad to be rid of them. I was afraid someone would find out I had the damned things and knock me in the head for them."

The elevator bell dinged and the doors rattled partway open, stalled and shuddered closed. The researcher swore and held the button in with his thumb. "Blasted thing. Sometimes you have to keep pressing the button."

Russ watched the performance with visible doubt. "Ummm, Chief? Maybe we ought to use the stairs."

"Good idea," Frost agreed, inordinately relieved. Before they could take more than a few steps toward the stairwell door, though, an ear-splitting klaxon went off. Heavy metal security doors slid down, cutting off the elevator and stairway exit.

"What in hell is *that*?" Frost shouted over the noise.

Dr. Bolle was frozen in place, a look of confusion on his face. "It's the containment breach alarm. Emergency lockdown has been initiated . . . but for the life of me I can't understand why. There should be nothing dangerous *in* containment."

The groan of metal under stress rose over the blare of the alarm. Hair standing up on the back of his neck, Frost whirled toward the sound. He stood momentarily transfixed at the sight of green, ivy-like tendrils forcing their way around the edges of the door to another lab down the hall. The spell was broken when the door burst off its hinges and slammed into the far wall, releasing a flood of greenery and several tall, tree-like figures into view. The creatures moved with an oddly fluid gait, like ice skaters. It could be considered graceful, even beautiful, if the skaters weren't so deadly.

"Shit! Nothing dangerous. Just a crapload of Nova Terran saplings!" Frost said.

"NO! Dr. Hartsturm is in there!" Bolle bolted forward, toward the green chaos at the other end of the corridor.

"Nonononono!" Frost shouted, jerking the researcher back by a handful of lab coat.

"Do *not* run toward Gaeans, man!" Russ said, taking hold of Bolle's flailing arms. "They'll get to you fast enough on their own."

Between them, they hustled the frantic scientist into his own laboratory and slammed the door against a volley of small, thorn-like projectiles.

Once the door closed, the doctor lost steam. He sagged against a worktable. "But, Hartsturm. . . ."

"Forget it, Doc. If your pal was in there with those saplings, there won't be enough of him left to worry about," Frost said, shooting the deadbolts home. Something solid hit the door from the other side. "Is there a lockdown for this room?"

"That button!" Bolle called over the blaring alarm. "The big orange square by the containment booth!"

The steel door bowed dangerously against its frame as Russ dove for the button and slapped it with an open palm. A solid steel shield clanged down behind the rolling door. The one at the front, however, didn't work so well. The barricade there dropped slightly lower than the middle point and went no farther. Russ slapped the button several more times. It did nothing.

Bolle whimpered. "Damn you, Hartsturm. Always too cheap to buy the good stuff."

"Note to self," Russ said. "Never trust my personal protection to the lowest bidder."

"Not helping, Russ," Frost growled.

"Sorry, Chief."

Swearing in frustration, Frost put his back against the side of the stasis unit. With a burst of effort, he shoved until it moved, screeching against the terrazzo floor. He kept pushing until the big machine covered the entire front entry, then, breathing hard, looked around for anything else to use. No good. Everything else was either bolted to the floor or not heavy enough to be useful. After a moment, he realized Dr. Bolle was staring at him. "What?"

"You're a Mod, aren't you? I should have realized earlier, given your height and build."

Frost said nothing.

The scientist nodded toward the big stasis cabinet. "That unit is one of the heaviest pieces in the lab. Took an entire crew to lug that monster in here, yet you slid it across the floor by yourself."

"Busted." Frost allowed a bitter laugh. "I would blame adrenaline, but I suppose there's no point. Didn't think a geneticist would have a problem with a genetically modified human."

"No, no, I don't," the researcher said hastily. "I've often thought about it, myself, but I . . . I know how painful those procedures can be. You're an even braver man than I thought, Mr. Frost."

"Not really. It was done to save my life. Since I was unconscious at the time, I didn't have much say in the matter." Beside him, the heavy storage unit shifted as tendrils worked their way through cracks and crevasses and around the machine. "Much as I'd like to discuss it with you, this isn't the time or place. Is there an individual release for the barricades? Something that would open one door but not all of them?"

"Looking for that right now, Chief," Russ said from across the room. "I'm jacked into the main server. Sifting through damage reports and life readings."

"And?"

"It ain't pretty. Looks like three saplings total. The good news is they're all busy trying to kick our door in at the moment."

Bolle looked hopeful. "What about the lab next door?"

"No life scans except sapling roots. Lots of roots."

"Then Dr. Hartsturm really is. . . ," Bolle gulped.

"Sorry, man. No human readings other than you and Dev."

During the exchange, Frost had been pacing the perimeter of the room. There wasn't much to find, but there *was* a fire extinguisher in the corner where the container shelves met the wall. He read the label and grinned. "CO2. We're in business."

Grabbing the tank from its cradle, he hurried over to

where tendrils were slithering under and actually lifting the makeshift barricade. He cut loose with a blast that fogged the air and coated the invasive greenery with white. The fibrils shriveled and pulled back.

"Ah!" Dr. Bolle exclaimed. "They don't like cold!"

"They aren't real fond of electricity, either, but neither will keep them away for long when they're set on a goal. This is a lousy time to ask, but what the hell were you guys doing out here?"

"We were studying the genetic structure of—"

"No. I mean what were you *really* doing? Nobody pays as much as you did unless you're doing something that might raise a couple eyebrows."

The researcher looked furtive, then seemed to give up. "We're cloning Nova Terrans. Especially the saplings. Their rate of growth would make them very valuable. Ummmmm . . . commercially."

Frost stared. "WHAAAT? Why? Those bastards will rip you in half sooner than look at you."

"We . . . that is Hartsturm . . . thought he'd found a way to mitigate that."

The door shook again as another mat of rootlets forced out from under the storage unit. Frost cut loose with another blast of the extinguisher, but the incursion didn't pull back as quickly as before. Snarling, he brought the base of the extinguisher down onto the thickest vine. The tendrils pulled back quickly, leaving a thin trail of sap in their wake. He looked over at the trembling researcher. "Yeah. I see how that worked out."

"He thought we could domesticate them. Like cattle . . . or sheep."

There wasn't much to say to that. Frost continued to

regard the geneticist as if he'd sprouted leaves himself until Russ broke in, "Chief — Dev, I found the protocols for the rolling door to this room. It leads to an outer hallway with a freight elevator and a stairwell, but we'll have to be fast. I can't override it for long."

Bolle and Frost were at the warehouse-style door before the synthoid had finished speaking, pulling at the lift chain, raising it to reveal the riveted steel plates behind it.

"Go for it!" Frost shouted.

Russ turned back to the computer interface. After a moment, there was a series of clanks and the grinding of gears as the heavy slab in front of them rose a full meter before stopping with a hiss and the stench of overloaded circuitry. Bolle needed no coaxing and was in the outer hall even before Frost. Russ, still at the command panel, took a running start and hit the floor in a slide like an old time baseball player stealing home. He made it through as the mechanisms gave up. The door fell, cracking the concrete floor with its impact.

"You okay?" Frost asked.

"I think so, but I'm gonna need a new jacket." The synthoid sat up slowly, fingers probing his left shoulder. Silvery liquid glistened on his fingertips. "And maybe a little first-aid."

Frost started toward his partner, but a loud crash from the room they'd just vacated stopped him in his tracks. That was followed by a shriek of protesting metal and another crash, then part of the wall dented outward. It was a large, square shape. Roughly the size of the stasis unit.

"Looks like they breached the front door," Russ observed.

Then there was another sound. A quieter one, almost

lost against the cacophony of the lockdown klaxon and the destruction in the room beyond. A sort of muffled whump. After a moment, another, shriller, alarm joined in.

Bolle moaned. "Wonderful. They must have ruptured some of the chemical containers. As if it could get much worse."

"What do you mean?" Frost looked up from tending his friend's shoulder. The injury wasn't serious and the healing function was already kicking in.

"That's the fire alarm," the scientist said in a flat tone.

Russ looked thoughtful. "The emergency protocols programmed into the building control system call for oxygen to be cut off in the affected areas."

Frost groaned. "And we're in an affected area."

"No, no," Russ said. "That might not be a bad thing. According to protocol, the only areas affected are the ones where the fire is. As long as the walls aren't breached, the halls would read as neutral."

"So we're good out here?"

"Maybe."

"I don't like 'maybe', Russ."

"We may not have to worry about that," Bolle said.

Frost didn't like his tone. "Why is that, Doc?"

"Remember how I said that Dr. Hartsturm was a cheap bastard?"

"Uhhhhh. Yeah."

"Well, he paid to reinforce the walls, but not the ceilings or floors."

Russ turned away from a panel he'd been examining. "So what you're saying is we don't have fire control, we have a chimney."

"If the fire breached the ceiling, I would say that was a

pretty accurate description, yes."

There was another rumble. This time from the center of the building somewhere below them. The corridor went black. The sudden absence of alarms was startling. After a few seconds, an ancient emergency light near the stairwell sign clicked on, illuminating the area with a weak, yellowish glow.

"And now no power." Frost said thumping his head on the wall behind him.

Russ turned back to whatever he was doing to the panel beside the stairway. "That's about the size of it, Chief."

Frost yelped and leaped to his feet. He touched the lab's wall cautiously, then pulled away, shaking his fingers. "Damn! We're definitely hotting up in there. I'd say the chimney theory wins."

He moved to the other side of the corridor. It was cooler, although he knew that was temporary. He could feel the heat from inside the burning lab even there. "On the up side," he said. "It's quieter now. The fire seems to have taken a toll on the saplings, too. At least they aren't banging on the wall any more. Of all the ways I'd imagined dying, being the main course for a Nova Terran barbecue was never in my top choices."

"The Nova Terrans *eat* people?" Bolle asked in sudden fear.

"Nah, I think they use humans for fertilizer," Russ said, peeling back the panel he'd been working on. "You know. *After* they rip your— WOO HOO! I popped the lock to the stairwell. Gimme a hand and I bet we can get out."

Several minutes and a few sliced fingers later, the lockdown gate was out of the way and the three of them pelted down the smoke-filled stairwell. The door that stood between them and freedom was a standard model that had no chance against Frost's boot. Fresh air rushed in, but that was a mixed blessing. Eyes streaming, they ran blindly, to get as much distance as possible between themselves and the burning building before oxygen and flame did what they did best.

When he could run no more, Frost dropped onto the scrubby pavement, gulped crisp desert air and looked back in time to see a mini fireball blossom from the open stairwell and a column of flame shoot through the roof of the complex. Russ, smeared with soot, sank to the ground beside him. For a while they sat, listening to the sirens approaching in the distance and the roar of flame.

"We lost the Doc," Russ said, nodding to the now-empty parking slot between the slogan-plastered road car and their own battered skimmer. To the west, a set of taillights shrank into the murky night, speeding away from them and the ABQ city-plex. "At least he didn't ask for his money back."

"He'd have to fight me for it," Frost said, pushing himself upright and striding for the skimmer. "He's got the right idea, though. We don't want to be around when the emergency responders get here. I don't want to answer questions any more than Bolle did."

"But, Chief," Russ said, falling in behind his partner. "What if those saplings are still—" He never finished his thought. The side of the building shuddered and collapsed inward, sending showers of sparks high into the sky.

"You were saying?"

"Never mind," Russ said, diving into his seat as the doors sealed and the mag-lift whined into life. "Where to? Someplace without Gaeans, I hope."

"I'm thinking north. I hear the Nova Terrans never got a real good foothold up around the Yukon and such."

"True. Very cold up that way."

XX SIW Goes **Platinum**

Frost nodded and pushed the throttle forward. The thrusters complained, but the battered vehicle lifted up and shot across the desert toward the highway.

"Meantime," he said, "you better see if you can get the solar heater working. I think we're gonna need it."

"And a new jacket?"

"And a new jacket."

"Right, Chief."

"I hate when you call me that."

Two Pots of Gold
Brenda Drexler

The town of Hank, Indiana is about as big as a speck of dust compared to the bigger cities in the state. Actually, Hank isn't really a city . . . more of a town, a really, small town, actually a tiny town, to give you a more exact description. The story is that the town was named by its first settlers when one fella said, "Well, here we are. What the Hank we going to call it?" and the other fella said, "Ok by me."

You've probably passed through this kind of community many times on the way to somewhere else, except you don't often know you're anywhere when you go through 'em.

Hank's the kind of place where everybody knows everybody and most people show up to one of the three churches most Sundays, or now and then.

And at least one of the churches has a big pitch-in dinner on any given Sunday, which most likely accounts for that being the kind of day when the pews are full and little kids are crawling around on the floor and getting whacked on their behinds by their daddies. It's good people, for the most part. Every town has its odd eggs to tolerate, and Hank is real good at tolerating, most of the time.

But the good town of Hank was having some problems. The town folk were in a real pickle about what to do to make things better since just about all the bad luck possible had been visited upon this community. The mill in the next town, which employs a lot of Hank's residents, had been threatening to close down, affecting, in a really bad way, a lot of the townsfolk. A larger town in the other direction had been threatening to just up and take Hank over. Not to mention the bad weather that made for bad crops. People could hardly get a good vegetable garden going this year.

Funny thing, even though a vegetable won't grow well in these parts, it's a known fact that one of the *sin* crops, marijuana, weed, pot . . . whatever you want to call it grows practically on its own, without no help. And it's a well-known fact that some people in our town have been known to grow some of it for their own use. The thing is, it seems to be the healthiest crop in Hank. So healthy that more and more folk were talking about making it legal. If California can do it, why the Hank couldn't Hank?

Of course, this sort of predicament was getting people all worried and riled up, talking gloom and doom, and such. Some folks were saying there was just too much sinning going on, and all the good-for-nothings had better get right with the Lord. Others didn't totally disagree with this argument, but didn't think it was fair to blame a few folks who are good most of the time, but have a few indiscretions in their pockets.

So that's why the town folk were gathering in Fred Jenkins' barn, being the biggest and soundest barn in the area, for a meeting that would likely run into the deep of night. A meeting like this, of such import, would usually end with the little kids sleeping on bales of Fred's hay while the bigger kids would be whooping and hollering around a bonfire they put together with the smaller branches that Fred had cut off some logs recently and wood from an old shed he knocked down.

Reverend Billy Bohannon, the highly respected pastor of the Hank Town Church of Christ United, was holding the only microphone available, which came from his wife's karaoke machine that he bought for her 40th birthday. He was standing atop of Fred's tractor that Fred had refused to move out of the barn, just in case it rained. Fred cleaned his tractor after every use and he wasn't going to let it get dirty because no one else had the pride to keep up their barns fit enough to have a town meeting.

Reverend Billy must have gotten into some of the church wine during the evening, or been around to Fred's kitchen where he keeps his private stock, because he wasn't holding anything back. Never saw him so rambunctious in his speaking, and the waving of his arms and pointing his finger left, right and middle of the whole room, meaning he's expecting everyone there to be listening.

"It's up to every last one of us . . . man, woman, and child to turn this all around, to make our community healthy again, even robust and alive, like it once was." He'd have to pause ever now and again for what he was saying to sink in. I could see neighbors eyeballing neighbors, shaking their heads one way or the other.

"What's he mean by *robust?*" Fred asked, turning to see Reverend Billy's wife, Louise, because she was standing right next to him. "I'm sorry Mrs. Louise. Didn't mean to sound offensive, just wondering." She didn't seem to notice Fred being there, much less care what he had to say. She was looking up at the Reverend with a sparkle in her eyes like it was the second coming, or something.

Then the Reverend continued. "What we got so far is a list of accusations, which we're going to throw in that bonfire out there, because we just don't have time for that kind of stuff. What we need are solutions, and we have a list of those, thank goodness, and thank all y'all for the ideas."

A lot of folk were looking perplexed at that, sort of screwing up their foreheads and looking around again . . . I suppose they were wondering who the y'all was. "Nobody asked me nothing," groused the town barber.

"Reverend," yelled one of the men in the crowd. "Ain't some of these ideas sort of sinful?"

"Well, now, Macon, thanks for bringing that up, 'cause that's a darn good thing to consider. We all know there are different ways to look at many of these ideas. So I'm suggesting that the town council, including the three pastors of our town's churches, get together tomorrow and choose what will work the best to revive our little town. We'll even have a backup plan if the first doesn't pan out . . . our ace in the hole, if you don't mind the reference to gambling. If we don't solve our own problems, then the larger cities around us are going to swallow us up and ruin us even more with their taxes, and more sinful doings than we could ever come up with on our own."

Out of nowhere, the Reverend Julius Moore . . . the pastor of the Disciples of Christ Church . . . was standing next to Reverend Bohannon, who was handing Julius the microphone like he didn't want to let go of it.

Now, I've heard my momma and pops talking sometimes, usually after they have a few swigs of the white lightning Pops keeps in mason jars, about how Reverend Moore and Reverend Bohannon, while they were just in middle school, would get in fights over the same pretty girl every daggum day. They sorta took turns giving each other black eyes. Course, that cute little girl's last name is Moore now. And the Reverend Billy seems okay with that, I guess, as he's married to Mrs. Louise. But I guess that'd be gossip if I said more about that.

"Folks, we been talking amongst ourselves whilst we listened to your concerns. Seems to us, from what we know, that what the town needs more than anything else is money and attention from the outside world. Now, there aren't many ways to make a lot of money in an area like ours without creating something Unique, LARGE."

Before long the barn was heating up. People were getting real excited, shuffling back and forth whispering amongst their neighbors and friends, some mouths hanging open in wonder, and such, with the way he used those last two words together to seem pretty special. "Now, I know," he paused to wait for the crowd to quiet down, just like in church, "that gambling doesn't seem like a Godly thing to consider, or the growing of a crop that the high-and-mighty government . . . that has no problem spending our tax money everywhere else but here . . . wants to say is illegal some places, but not others. These are desperate times. And, I think we have a right to use the resources the Good Lord has given us."

He sure enough paused again, because there were hands waving and voices yelling, and some bad things said about the government spending our money. Drops of sweat was dripping off some noses and foreheads. Men and women were wiping their brows and licking their lips. The Reverend held up his hands and the room got quiet, all eyes on him. "You, the good people of our town, can make anything work if we all do it together." He just waited and nodded his head until the clapping and the roar of agreement died down again.

"Also, every last one of our citizens, who are citizens at

this very moment, and their descendants will reap the financial benefits if we choose one or more of these ideas. Think about it, folks. It's mind-boggling."

He stepped aside and handed the microphone to the pastor of the Hank Town Universal Baptist Church of the Risen Lord and Savior of All, Reverend Josiah Baker, as he also managed to find his place atop Fred's shiny tractor. "Dearly beloved. I know the kind of good people you are: God-fearing family folk, who only want to do the right thing any day of the week. But you also know that you must do something different to survive, or our little town will disappear like we were never here. And you want to do the *RIGHT* thing. So, here's what we have come up with to make sure we are being just and fair and such." Another pause. Not a sound except for some heavy breathing, just quiet waiting. Except for the rowdy teenagers outside.

"Here's our plan. Everyone here, everyone who lives in our town, has to attend at services this Sunday. Can't be one empty spot on a pew, can't be one single person staying home, no matter what is happening. If we have a tornado or your mare decides to drop a foal . . . no excuse. We'll pray and sing, and we'll wait for a sign. If we pray long enough and hard enough and all together, there will be a sign. And if it's a positive sign we'll go through with the plans that we decide on tomorrow, most likely opening a casino that will belong to this town, these people. Lord knows we have a lot of good-for-nothing dirt to build on." He was waving his arms in the air from one side of the barn to the other. There was a mix of clapping and mumbling in the crowd. Others were moving in motion with the preacher, making me a little scared they would be speaking in tongues any minute.

"What do we do if it's a negative sign, Rev?"

"What if we don't get everyone in church at the same time?"

"We'll know when we see the sign. And if we can't get every single person here into church this Sunday, then I bet anything that the rest of you will figure out a way to get them into church by the next Sunday. Our children's future depends on it."

"Tell you what," yelled out Fred, "don't anybody here better be messing with my kid's future. Be in church this Sunday, is all I got to say."

There was a lot of mumbling in agreement. And I tell you, anyone would be plum stupid to not show up. Hard telling what the town folk might do to get them in church. Most of 'em were fired up for some money-making venture to save our community. So, we waited for Sunday services with deep anxiety and maybe some trepidation.

Now, I have to admit that I was just too curious to wait till Sunday services, especially when the reverends stated that they would be meeting to talk more about what kind of law our town might be breaking.

So, I just happened to volunteer to clean the town hall community building, where they would all meet to decide the town's fate, so I could get the skinny on this deal. I learned some interesting stuff, I guess no one else in town knew. I had no idea, before this day, the three churches, most notably the three pastors had bought up some rather large parcels of land, and wanted to put them to use real soon.

People of Hank noted that the sky looked mighty dreary for the next few days . . . lightning storms, high winds, and hail. Some folks were thinking that the town was already getting its sign and it wasn't a good one.

By the time Sunday church services rolled around most folks were feeling as gloomy as the sky looked. Still, they warned the possible holdouts that they better have their bottoms sitting on a pew, or else.

It rained so hard that most everyone was soaked to the skin by the time they made their way into their chosen church that Sunday morning, approximately at 9 in the am. Every last person was accounted for, even old Jake, the only barber in town, and the only declared agnostic I know of, and darned if he didn't have one ugly black eye that he wouldn't explain to nobody. He came in with Eugene. Most of Eugene's family happens to work at that old mill in the next town, the one that was threatening to close down.

The preacher was preaching, the organ playing and everyone singing the regular hymns. But the attendees just weren't feeling it. They were thinking for sure that there was no chance of a good sign this day that would help them and their town to survive. But they kept on singing.

Over in Reverend Billy Bohannon's (that's where I go), he got up and was wildly leading the churchgoers to raise their voices in song until they drowned out the rain. I heard that pretty much the same was happening at the other churches, too. It was surely something to make people proud, even if it was wet and gray outside.

People will talk about that day for many years to their sleepy kids on the bales of hay and to their grandchildren that aren't even born yet. It's truly hard to imagine how far and wide the news of what happened in Hank that day would travel. But, I tell you, it was a sight like none other.

When clouds of dust rained down from the church rafters because of the vibration from the loudest singing ever heard, and the people were waving their hands in the air, and some were crying with uncontrollable joy, the sky opened up and sent the most beautiful colors in through the church windows ever seen before.

The church hushed. The town became quiet. Not even a dog barking or a squirrel screeching in a tree could be heard. The church doors flung open and everyone flowed out to the streets. The bright sun over that way and deep blue skies the other and the most amazing double rainbow ever seen or heard of. I'm not talking about a regular rainbow, here, no way. I'm talking two double rainbows that crisscrossed each other to look like a stained glass window in the sky that only could be made in heaven. It brought tears to every eye that saw it, no doubt.

People were hugging, some dropping to their knees. Eventually everyone from all three churches was milling around hugging and shaking hands. No more rain. The ground was drying up fast, making it a lot better for our big pitch-in, already planned to either mourn or praise the day.

Reverend Bohannon, with his wife's microphone again, said, "Brothers and sisters. This is indeed a blessed day for all of us, a sign never seen before by anyone here, and a sign maybe never seen again or in our lifetimes. We are on our way to enjoying untold prosperity together. We got our sign as far as I'm concerned. Let's eat."

"I was rather partial to the other idea brought up, myself," complained, Aileen, Fred's wife, who owned the town bakery, to Eugene's wife. "Think I'll still add specialty brownies and cookies to my menu."

"I'll surely buy a heap of 'em," said, Nora. "You bake like nobody's business, honey."

"You betcha . . . won't be no body's business unless they're paying for them." She nudged Nora and they both giggled.

Now, I love the town of Hank, done all my growing and learning here, but, fact is, I heard every word spoken in that little meeting of the prominent and powerful people in this whole area. And I knew things that the whole of the town-folk knew nothing about.

The highly respected bunch of people in that meeting had watched the weather closely, and expected thunder and lightning, and even got more rainbow than they ever expected. But they were cunning men, reverends and all, and weren't about to totally count on the thunderstorm delivering them down the path of righteous gambling. The rest of the plan included a sinful person showing up at each church full of repentance at the exact same moment, and being baptized and saved all at once. Too bad they weren't needed, after all. That double/double rainbow was enough for us. I expect when I'm older, I'll be getting me a job at our new casino.

Contributors

The Southern Indiana Writers Group has been more-or-less together since 1992. We began meeting monthly in a conference room in a local hospital. We now meet weekly to exchange information and expertise on everything from computers to poetry. The group also serves as a critique forum (in the same sense that a pack of wolves serves as food critics). Membership is limited, but visitors are welcome, and have been known to fit in so well they become members against their better judgment.

Bonnie Abraham After twenty-five plus years of writing letters disqualifying people from Unemployment Benefits, she retired in order to write something more pleasant. She writes short stories (many with Biblical themes), poetry and devotionals. Currently, she resides in Corydon with her mother's ghost.

Jan Wolanin Alexander retired science teacher married to a biology professor, mother of 10 fur-children: 1 horse, 4 dogs, and 5 cats, custom horsehair jewelry maker, part-time dog kennel worker, writer of horse tales, trail rider.

Marian Allen lives in a big house in a little wood, which is not the only difference between Allen and Laura Ingels Wilder. She has published stories in print and on-line magazines, including Marion Zimmer Bradley's FANTASY Magazine, The Phone Book, PanGaia and Oceans of the Mind. She blogs at marianallen.com.

Contributors

Brenda Drexler was a high school, middle school, GED and college English teacher in a past life. After some major life changes and a root canal, she returned to school to become a psychotherapist. She is currently teaching at a local community college and proudly calling herself a writer. She is an avid reader of a variety of genres. The work she is most proud of includes three articles published in a local newspaper and an anonymous letter to a senior officer on an Army post (Let's keep that little secret to ourselves). Her book of short stories, Four Shorts for Your Bucket List, can be found at Lulu.com and Amazon.com. She recently completed her first novel, Gracie and Marge: Kicking the Bucket Together, with some absolutely zany characters that you will love at first sight. It can be found at CreateSpace and Amazon.com. Brenda is thankful for the feedback of her husband, sisters and friends after they proofread her works in progress. She's indebted to the good people of SIW for their keen eyes in perusing the written word and their blunt honesty. (She plans to use that last sentence when she wins an Oscar or Emmy, or something.)

Ginny Fleming considers herself to be foremost a screenwriter, as this is her favorite media. Because nobody thought to tell her she couldn't, after optioning 3 scripts for the unsold ensemble sitcom "*Tia*" (any producers reading this?), Fleming dived head-first into the shark-infested mulligan stew (How's that for mixing metaphors?) that is Hollywood scriptwriting. Fleming's take on hysterical fantasy (funny, that is), a novel she likes to call *Dragonsayver* (when she's not calling it Marvin), is a "Shrek-like" novel just begging to be made into an animated film (Fleming wonders if she should shove a tin cup in its hand and drop it on a busy intersection). Besides her annual contribution to SIW anthology and a brief appearance in the Louisville Courier-Journal, Fleming is busy finding a home for *Keys of Illusion*, a Romantic/Suspense novel filled with magic, scuba, fantasy, a bunch of lavender stuff and little bit of sex. Multiple scripts are always in the works whenever Fleming manages to "channel" Jimmy Buffett, her "Muse" (Yeah, she knows Jimmy's not dead — Hopes for his continued good health, in fact — That just makes him easier to channel).

Andrea Gilbey is the most south-eastern member of the group – south-east England, that is.

She visits the group as often as she can to add some British colour, (because that's how they spell it over there), whenever she can get leave from her day job as a footwear technologist. (Motto – breaking shoes so you don't have to.)

Andrea has published five illustrated children's books for pre-schoolers and upwards and, with SIW colleague Ginny Fleming, worked on the Written In Our Hearts Cookbook in aid of the Davy Jones Equine Memorial Foundation.

She is currently working on a sequel to her first novel, Bottletops For Battleships, which is set in wartime England.

Andrea lives in leafy Hertfordshire with her two cats.

T Lee Harris is a scribbler of the lowest order. Not only does she pen lies about people who don't exist, but she draws pictures of them as well. Harris has also been known to aid and abet others by putting their scribblings into book form and even going so far as to devise covers for these publications. She claims she went to school to learn these things, but that shouldn't be held against anyone.

Harris is, in turn, aided and abetted by others in her assaults against literature. Among these accomplices are Per Bastet Publications, who have shamelessly published her untruths about an ancient Egyptian scribe and a magic temple cat and most recently spread her prevarications about a former football player and a 200 year-old vampire turned international law enforcement agents. Also implicated are Untreed Reads, who have promulgated her lies about a retired spy who keeps getting mixed up in other people's business, and the Southern Indiana Writers' Group — possibly the worst offenders of all — who have repeatedly permitted her to commit her acts of literary vandalism with their Indian Creek Anthology Series.

There are suspicions that Harris is committing another novel or two, but this has yet to be confirmed.

Michele Hubler acquired a motto as the usual overconfident teenager: "It (it being anything that she didn't know how to do) can't be that hard."

She has since found a few things that were indeed that hard, such as mothering a son, attending graduate school in instructional design, getting a job with Xerox, and now, writing humor, fantasy and other odd stories. But as a rule, the motto has served her well.

Brett Alan Sanders is a writer, translator, and recently retired teacher living in Tell City, Indiana. He earned a BA in Spanish (with an English minor) at Indiana University and an MALS at the University of Southern Indiana. He has been a contributing writer at Tertulia Magazine, where for "Tertullian's Blog" he wrote the occasional column "Arte Retórica," and a former columnist for the Perry County (IN) News. In addition he served a brief stint as managing editor at New Works Review and has translated for the literary-arts website suelta. He has published original essays, fiction, and literary translations in a variety of journals including Hunger Mountain, Artful Dodge, The Antigonish Review, Confluence: The Journal of Graduate Liberal Studies, and Rosebud. He has also published a YA novella (A Bride Called Freedom, Ediciones Nuevo Espacio, 2003) and two book-length translations from the work of Buenos Aires writer María Rosa Lojo (Awaiting the Green Morning, Host Publications, 2008; Passionate Nomads, Aliform Publications, 2011). He may be contacted via his website/blog at www.brettalansanders.wordpress.com.